SMALL TOWN BLUES

"Isn't it awful about Manly Richards?"

"What about Manly Richards?"

Ladawn's next statement cut off my thoughts. "He's dead—he was murdered. They didn't release his name until late last night because they couldn't find that wife of his."

Even though reporters are supposed to keep an open mind, I quickly decided on the hard-to-find wife as the culprit. "So have they arrested her?" I said.

"Oh, no. And evidently, Belinda Bullard, the head aerobic instructor at the Iron Body Health Club, has been having private horizontal aerobic time with Manly Richards."

I wondered if my sister Angel had had any idea Manly was otherwise involved.

ANGEL'S AURA

Brenda Jernigan

HarperPaperbacks
A Division of HarperCollinsPublishers

This is a work of fiction. The characters, incidents, and dialogues are products of the author's imagination and are not to be construed as real. Any resemblance to actual events or persons, living or dead, is entirely coincidental.

HarperPaperbacks   *A Division of* HarperCollins*Publishers*
10 East 53rd Street, New York, N.Y. 10022

Cover illustration by Jeff Walker

First printing: April 1995

Printed in the United States of America

HarperPaperbacks, HarperMonogram, and colophon are trademarks of HarperCollins*Publishers*

❖ 10 9 8 7 6 5 4 3 2

For Katherine and Benjamin,
my good karma rolled into two souls.

I am grateful to my parents, Raymond and Jean Jernigan, for reasons too numerous to name here, not the least of which is raising me in a family that tells wonderful stories. A special thanks to my sister, Becky Hardee, for seeing life in her own special way. And to the others who have supported this effort, Tommy Hardee, Amanda Hardee, Michael Hardee, Doug and Cynthia Jernigan, and Katherine and Benjamin Chesson.

I wish to acknowledge the help of Mark Jernigan, attorney at law, Sonja Ford, sports medicine specialist, and Larry Knott, Deputy Director, Harnett County Sheriff's Department, for his tour of the Harnett County Correctional Facility. Any errors in the material presented are my own and not the result of their assistance.

For reading and rereading, my thanks to Marlynn Brock and Schelli Barbaro Whitehouse.

ANGEL'S AURA

1

au•ra (OR ə) *n.* **1.** An invisible emanation or exhalation. **2.** A distinctive air or quality.

Don't go looking for books on psychics at Book Universe. It doesn't have them. I know because I've looked. Drove all the way to Raleigh to find out. What Book Universe had were those big brown and red signs above every section of books for easy reference. I had already ruled out the cooking, art, pet care, and business sections, though if you asked Edgar he'd say I've been cooking with psychic power for years (I just throw in whatever the spirits move me to). And, to be honest with you, with the amount of money my sister Angel had been spending with Madame Zsa Zsa, there ought to have been at least one book in the business section on the subject.

Angel is my youngest sister. As she was the baby, Mama and Daddy always spoiled her terribly. No doubt, that is what led to her going through husbands about as fast as she did hair colors. Edgar says Miss Clairol died a millionaire on account of Angel. Once, when she dated a Ph.D. candidate from Chapel Hill, he was going to do a thesis correlating her hair color changes with the greenhouse effect or some such phenomenon. They broke up after Angel realized that doctor's degree he was getting didn't mean she had hooked an open heart surgeon. Her sudden attachment to Madame Zsa Zsa was what had me worried. Madame Zsa Zsa had seen what she called "unnatural red" in Angel's karma, and it was taking every penny Angel had collected on her last husband Larry's death benefits to try to rid herself of it. Meanwhile, I pointed out to Angel that Madame Zsa Zsa was getting a lot of very natural green.

I was getting ready to move to the medical section when Idaleen Newsome rounded the corner. The very reason I was not in the Martinsboro Public Library at that exact minute and doggone if she wasn't right there in Book Universe.

Idaleen Newsome, the Martinsboro librarian, is married to Purdy Newsome's first cousin, Rayford. Purdy is my boss down at *The Martinsboro News Herald*. I've been working there part-time as a reporter since Jason, my youngest, went off to school. Besides being one of the leading authorities on books and poetry in the Martinsboro area and having a reading salon in her living room once a month (a reading salon being different than a hair salon because everyone has already had their hair done when they go to the reading salon and gossip runs in a more literary vein), besides all that, Idaleen has got a nose to know, if you catch my drift. I ruled the library out because I figured first she'd smile and nod that primly permed head of hers at me and then she'd lean over the front counter and whisper, "May I help you?" in her official librarian's voice. I'd shake my head no and she'd wait until I had pulled a book from the shelf, sat down, and started reading it and then would announce in a quiet whisper to the other staff that she needed to go to the ladies' room. Before you could shake a stick, she'd be looking over my back trying to read what was on the printed page I was holding.

Well, I thought to myself, *Barbara Gail Upchurch, sometimes it just doesn't pay to try to be too tricky.*

"Idaleen, imagine meeting you here. It must be great minds think alike. How's Rayford?"

"My goodness, Barbara Gail, what a pleasant surprise!"

It was then I noticed the flush on Idaleen's neck creeping up towards her face like the red dye in the celery stick in Melissa's fifth grade science project. I glanced down as the titles *How to Make Love with Your Husband for the Rest of Your Life* and *The Sensuous Woman* disappeared from view.

"Working hard at Morganite, but he's fine, very fine."

I bet he is, with books like that around the house, I thought. When Edgar and I got married fifteen years ago we rented a house from Old Man Turlington. Afternoons I'd stop by and see Mrs. Turlington on the way back from Campbell College, where I was a day student finishing my degree. Mrs. Thelma and I would talk while she had her afternoon toddy. She always told me, "Keep a man happy in bed and at the table and you'll never have to worry about his wandering." Lord knows what Old Man Turlington told Edgar would make me happy. I suppose something like leaving his dirty laundry on the floor. Edgar has always had the deepest respect for his elders.

Idaleen quickly went on the offensive. "I hear Angel is back in town."

"Yes, Idaleen, she's been back about two months now."

"Lord have mercy, Barbara, you never pass along the news to me. I'd have never known she was back if Wanda Perry hadn't told me she saw her out at the Bar-B-Q Barn with that Manly Richards a few nights ago. You know Manly; he runs that Iron Body Health Club off Erwin Road. Of course, Wanda thought for sure she'd heard he was married. But I told her, 'Oh go on, Wanda, you know Angel Larue wouldn't be running around with a married man in public. She's not that wild, and she is certainly not desperate.'"

So I'm smiling at Idaleen in the aisle of the Book Universe like it's every day someone who is not even a blood relation tells you your younger sister is carrying on with a married man. I should have known. I mean, Angel was just one of those women. A mass of blonde hair (the shade of the month), tight jeans, and high heels except when she waitresses over at Johnson's Truck Stop off 95. She is never without a crowd of men around her. Her man trouble started early in life, when she got sent home from kindergarten because the teacher found her at naptime on a little boy's mat kissing him. She claimed he promised her a new hula hoop.

I must admit I am a tad jealous since Angel trots off to the Iron Body Health Club in spandex looking like a million dollars while I slink off to the V.F.W. building three nights a week for Jazzercise in an oversize sweatshirt and sweatpants looking like change from a dollar that bought a Big Tee Burger and fries at the Dairy Queen. I wouldn't want anybody to be able to tell what's bag or what's sag.

But, Angel's looks are no excuse. If she thought she was above the moral code the rest of us live by, she should have been a politician.

Bad enough I was already wasting my time looking for a book to outsmart Madame Zsa Zsa so close to the holidays, when I had presents to buy and the Chamber of Commerce Christmas parade to plan, but, right there in the craft aisle, I found out we had the "scarlet woman" in the family.

And if I wasn't all ready to have a little "come-to-Jesus" meeting with Angel over her conduct of late, her choice of men was enough to decide me on one. Manly Richards was relatively new in town, but he was slimier than any frog Jason ever brought home from the creek below the house. "The spandex studmuffin," is what the college girls at the church all called him when they were home for Thanksgiving. I heard that from Misty Jane, daughter of my oldest sister, Vicki. They were all pretty sure he was married, though no one had seen the wife in question. The visitation committee from the church called on him at the club, but never could get any significant information out of him, not even whether he was saved or not. If he was, they felt it was definitely a matter of the Lord's infinite grace at that point.

Well, anyway, Idaleen and I stood in the bookstore that afternoon smiling saccharin smiles at one another, having no way of knowing that, saved or not, married or not, Manly Richards was knocked on the head, dead on the floor of his health club. He had pumped his last iron.

2

kar•ma (KAHR mə) *n*. **1.** The spiritual force generated by one's actions, which determines one's reincarnated situation. **2.** Loosely, fate.

    My sister Vicki and I were celebrating her birthday the next day when we heard about the arrest. Every year I treat Vicki to lunch at the Victorian Room on her birthday. After all, what are sisters for?

Vicki has a full ten years on me. She is forty-five. I'm thirty-five. She doesn't show her age at all. Makes me crazy. Her face, with its smooth complexion and round cheeks, looks like it belongs to someone a good ten years younger. Edgar says the extra twenty-five pounds she carries on account of Daddy's family genes are what causes her face to be so smooth. I've maintained my 135 over the years, though, in all honesty, those 135 pounds seem to be shifting around on me. The only exceptions to this were pregnancy and when

Edgar and I were newlyweds. I finished my degree despite everybody in Edgar's family constantly asking me why I needed a college degree; they said I should be happy tending to Edgar's needs and raising a family. They were always making some remark about my weight gain when we visited, hoping I would announce a baby on the way instead of just too many Coca-Colas and Zero bars at the student union.

Of course, I'm here to tell you Edgar Upchurch never missed a meal the whole time I finished my education, but his mama was sure I was feeding him sandwiches.

Sandwiches are ranked right up there with the communists in Mrs. Upchurch's opinion. Forget famine, war, and pestilence, the modern world is going to hell in a handbasket because families are having to eat sandwiches.

On the other hand, Vicki got married right out of high school and had Misty Jane when she was nineteen. Vicki doesn't age much, but, unfortunately for her, she got her taste in clothing from Mama's sister Louise. Fond of those pom-poms people once used to edge their curtains, Louise doesn't make a fashion statement—it's much more like a scream. At lunch that day, Vicki was dressed in a tight knit dress with horizontal stripes of brown and black that made her look like an overstuffed sausage that had been browned on the grill. Her brunette hair was neatly arranged to form a tight dark bubble around her face.

We each had the day's special, Ladawn Pittman's famous chicken pie. The flakiness of her pie crust is always an easy half hour of discussion at any Ladies' Auxiliary meeting. I've made up my mind that I'll never tell a soul I once saw her stuffing a whole bag of those Pillsbury refrigerator pie crust boxes into a trash can in the kitchen of the Victorian Room.

Ladawn is the owner of the Victorian Room. We've worked on several Chamber of Commerce committees together, and Ladawn has handled the Events Committee three years running. This year I'm co-chairing the Christmas Parade Committee with her.

Edgar has been threatening me with divorce because I have made him go with me to every Christmas parade within a one-hundred-mile radius this year. I told him I take my civic responsibilities very seriously and no one but no one is going to be able to say that Barbara Gail Upchurch did not put on the greatest move-over-Macy's parade that Martinsboro has ever seen. I reminded him that we all suffer through deer season and bird season and turkey season without so much as a grump. We endure stories of hunting episodes that last longer than the actual events, so if he has to watch a few measly parades with oversize baton twirlers in stretch-blue polyester, beauty queens and kings that only a mother could love, and bands whose idea of good Christmas music is "Grandma Got Run Over by a Reindeer," well, that's the way the mop flops sometimes.

Over the chicken pie, I told Vicki about my day on Monday. After my encounter with Idaleen at Book Universe, I had gone to pick up Melissa and Jason at Busy Buddies Day Care. Patsy Lockamy, the owner, met me at the front door. Patsy's rather voracious love of gossip has led Edgar to refer to the center as "Busybodies" Day Care. Edgar won't think he is so cute when one of the children calls her that to her face.

"I hear Angel and Manly Richards were out at the Bar-B-Q Barn the other night," Patsy said.

At that point, I had heard all of that little story about Angel that I was interested in hearing except from Angel herself, so I did a rather unchristian thing.

"Did they ever indict your minister on those charges of making harassing phone calls to congregation members?"

Patsy felt a sudden urge to go answer the ringing telephone. I proceeded on down the hall, wondering how Wanda Perry could manage to spread news so fast, hold down a full-time job, and raise three children. I was going to have to get her to speak to the Ladies' Auxiliary on the secrets of time management.

I had tried to reach Angel from the time I got home until Edgar and I left to take an engineer who is visiting at the mill to dinner in Raleigh. "No luck," I told Vicki. She and I needed a strategy. We decided that it was time for a little church chat among sisters. Angel obviously needed to understand that she was socially embarrassing herself with this Manly Richards thing, and if she wasn't careful Madame Zsa Zsa would lead her down the path to financial embarrassment as well. I hated getting mixed up in it, but Angel was famous for waiting until things fell down around her and then running to one of us to get her out. Mama and Daddy were getting too old to deal with a perpetual teenager. Once after she got Mama and Daddy out in the middle of the night to bail her out of jail, we had a huge fight. I explained to her that she needed to grow up and leave Mama and Daddy alone. She agreed, and started calling me when she was a victim of circumstances, which she frequently was. If you could catch her before she got on a roll you were less likely to get flattened by her.

Moving on to the New York-style cheesecake, Vicki and I had a discussion about Misty Jane. Vicki dabbed her eyes. "I think poor Misty Jane has gotten herself into a fit of nerves over this problem at the church."

The problem at the church concerned Misty Jane's placement in Sunday School. Misty Jane is in the College and Career Class; she commuted to Peace College for two years and received her degree in business. Her high school and college performances were fairly mediocre. In fact, I don't much like to admit it, since she is flesh and blood and everything, but poor Misty Jane is fairly mediocre herself. Her biggest claim to fame involved the Miss Martinsboro Christian Young Miss Pageant. She was crowned first runner-up, mostly because in the costume portion of the pageant she dressed herself as a Holy Bible in an outfit she made herself. Everyone agreed it was stunning. She was awarded the title several months later, when Suzanne Minchew was disqualified because several portions of her diary were circulating around various circles of teenagers in Martinsboro and had some rather unchristian portions.

I reported the story for the *News Herald* and I don't mind telling you that diary was something. I thought about subtitling my article "Suzanne Does Martinsboro." Purdy wouldn't let me, since we are a family newspaper, but I did keep going in his office and finding him with his nose stuck in her diary. Every time, he would turn a little red, slam the book, and mutter something about needing to stay on top of the news.

After college, Misty Jane took a position in the

billing office over at Northern Harnett Hospital. Since that time she'd had no offers of marriage and only an occasional date, which had disheartened her, a twenty-five-year-old woman with marriage as her single goal. This being the case, Misty Jane is by far and away the oldest member of the College and Career Class in recorded church history; her only option is to move up to the Hope Class, filled with "unclaimed blessings." Edgar says this class is aptly named because the women continue to hope long after all rational avenues have been exhausted. Misty Jane was refusing to move up. I didn't much blame her. We had this same trouble with Edgar's mom a few years ago. Mrs. Upchurch refused to promote out of the Fidelis Sunday School Class, which goes from sixty to sixty-five years of age. The next step was the Koinonia Class. The sign on the door said KOINONIA CLASS 65 YRS—. Clearly, the next promotion was heaven. Mrs. Upchurch could not be budged. In the same way, Misty Jane saw the Hope Class as an eternal consignment to spinsterhood.

"Vicki, it will all work out. Misty Jane is going to meet some nice young man or, Lord forbid, write a new computer program for hospitals to use in patient billing. She'll become independently wealthy, take young lovers when she feels like it, and forget all about getting married."

Vicki blushed at the mention of young lovers. "I think Joshua Merriwether might be interested in her."

She had a much better chance with the computer program, I thought. Joshua Merriwether was the newest family physician in Harnett County. He had raised himself up from the poverty the rest of his family still lived in over in the southern part of the county. His family was so prolific the family tree looked more like kudzu than an oak. The state of North Carolina had paid for his schooling in return for several years of work in a rural area. He had several clinics in outlying towns and a big clinic in Martinsboro. He provided health care, courtesy of the state, for a portion of the indigent population, but despite his big black BMW and his blond curly hair, I was unimpressed. I'd had to interview him for the *News Herald* when he first came back to town. Best I could tell, he wasn't doing anything to help out anybody else in his family. He would have been sorely disappointed if he had realized that, when he kept referring to his "Beamer," I thought he was talking about a flashlight.

I finished off my cheesecake as Vicki outlined a master plan to snag Dr. Joshua Merriwether's attention. With each bite of cheesecake, I was trying to think of a kind way of telling her that every mother in Harnett County, and a few in Johnston County, were after the good doctor.

Ladawn Pittman stopped by to check on us and refill our iced tea. She wore a khaki skirt, Indian-print blouse, and turquoise on her ears, neck, and arms. Collecting antique turquoise jewelry was her hobby. She was the only woman I knew who had jewelry with a pedigree. She wore her blonde hair in a bun at her neck, the top and sides pulled back to accentuate her angular face and high cheekbones.

"Isn't is awful about Manly Richards?" she said.

"What about Manly Richards?" My first thought was that Ladawn, whom I always thought of as a tasteful individual, was going to tell us about Angel and Manly. That thought was cut short by her next statement.

"He's dead."

Vicki made a sympathetic little cooing sound, "An accident?"

Ladawn put the tea pitcher down on the table. "Only if he accidently got in the way of the barbell somebody else was supposed to get hit in the head with. He was murdered in his office over at the health club."

"That's awful. When did they find him?" I was already worrying about Angel and how she was going to take all this.

"Yesterday morning, but they didn't release his name until late last night. They couldn't find that wife of his. When she finally showed up they say she reeked of alcohol and swore she'd been at the mall in Fayetteville all day." Ladawn rolled her eyes.

"I can't believe I missed all this. I was running around Raleigh all day looking for a book for Angel, then Edgar and I were in Raleigh last night for dinner."

"Well, what I didn't already know was filled in for me by Norton Maxwell when I stopped by the Dash Mart for gas on my way to the restaurant this morning," Ladawn said.

We all laughed. Norton was not one to keep secrets.

Even though reporters are supposed to keep an open mind, I had already decided on the hard-to-find wife.

"So have they arrested the wife?" I reached over and nipped a corner of Vicki's cheesecake with my fork, a bad habit of mine since childhood.

"Oh, no, and from what Bubba tells me they're going to have trouble narrowing it down to what woman actually killed him."

Bubba Pittman was Ladawn's son. He had played

football at East Carolina University and was now home trying to get in shape to try out for a walk-on spot with the pros.

The bite of cheesecake felt like it was stuck in my throat. "Really? What did he say?"

"Evidently, Belinda Bullard, who is the head aerobic instructor over at the Iron Body, was having private horizontal aerobic time with Manly Richards," Ladawn said.

"Is that right?" As I watched a wedge of lemon bob to the top of my iced tea, I wondered if Angel had any idea Manly was otherwise involved. I was irritated that, with her ability to have her choice of men, she seemed drawn to the ones that were like rats, happiest when they were up to their ears in garbage.

When I tuned back in to the conversation, Ladawn had asked Vicki how Joe Dan, Martin, and Misty Jane were doing. Martin is Vicki's eighteen-year-old, in his senior year at Martinsboro High. Joe Dan is Vicki's husband of almost twenty-seven years. It's a wonder to me how Vicki stays sane. Joe Dan hasn't ever had a day in his life when he isn't on the verge of a heart attack, to hear him tell it. His poor health (passed down from his father, who died at age fifty-seven of a heart attack) is enough to keep Joe Dan from helping around the house. Inside or out. Don't get me wrong, you won't catch Edgar Upchurch dusting or working on the laundry unless he's really in the dog house. Then he pays the children to clean so all he has to do is supervise. But not only does Joe Dan not do anything in the house, he doesn't do the yard work, or look after the vehicles, or even grill out, for gosh sake. Poor Vicki is stuck with it all. Best I can tell, his heart allows him to do only two things since he took early retirement from the mill: talk and fish.

Ladawn turned to me. "Before I forget, Barbara, Mitchell Hardison called for you a while ago. I told him you were here, but before I could say anything else, he hung up."

Mitchell was one of two full-time reporters at the *News Herald*. He was in his twenties and highly excitable. Wanting badly to make a name for himself, he followed every instruction of Purdy's down to the letter. I told him the only name that would make for him was "behind kisser."

"I bet Purdy wants me to work today on account of this murder, and I told him I wouldn't be available. That's what part-time means: part-time. If I wanted to be full-time, I would have said full-time. Purdy's glad enough to pay me a part-time salary."

Ladawn went off to check on the other customers and Vicki picked up her coat. She's been with the county manager's office almost twelve years now, and, even though she was head of the secretarial hierarchy, she thought taking lunches longer than an hour set a bad example, even on your birthday. Everywhere else she flitted around, but in the secretarial pool she ruled like Attila the Hun. We were almost at the door when Mitchell Hardison opened it and burst through with such commotion and agitation that he looked like a reject from a Richard Simmons video. I expected his weight loss success to flash on the screen in front of him. Gasping for breath and holding his side, he grabbed my arm.

"It's Manly Richards. Purdy said to find you."

"I know he's dead and Purdy is just going to have

to get someone else to cover it." I put my hand out to steady him. Purdy was bad for wanting me to go to work at the drop of a hat. "Melissa, Jason, and Becky have dentist appointments. You have no idea how hard it is to get three appointments at Dr. Nance's office on the same afternoon."

Mitchell looked confused. He gave me one of those looks like a mechanic gives you when you try and explain what's wrong with your car. Makes you want to say, "Me Jane, you Tarzan."

"I think I saw Chief Spivey arrest Angel."

I heard Vicki moan and out of the corner of my eye saw her sink back into her chair.

That's how it always worked. She fell apart and I kept my cool to deal with a crisis. Angel was different; she never had any idea there was a crisis. That's what you were there for anyway, to handle it. I love them to death, but one time I want to say to them, "Okay, this time I'll fall apart and y'all take this one." Everybody thinks I'm overloaded with those "inner strength" genes. I guess since Vicki lives with a family of individuals whose mental health is as fragile as glass Christmas ornaments, it's only fair she gets to fall apart when I'm around. After all, I have Edgar, who, compared to Joe Dan Macauley, looks like Robert Redford and John Wayne all rolled up together.

"Well, Mitchell, was it an arrest or not? I mean, are we talking about handcuffs and Miranda rights or are we not? For Pete's sake, you are supposed to be a reporter!"

"All I know is when she was getting into the patrol car, actually it was the chief's car, J.C. had his hand on Angel's elbow, sort of helping and sort of pushing her into the car. I asked politely, 'Excuse me, J.C., can this be considered a landmark arrest in the Manly Richards case?' He pushed me aside and said no comment. I am considering filing a suit. This is a thirty-one-point-weave oxford-cloth shirt and it's ruined.'"

Sometimes I think all that fizz in Mitchell's Perrier goes straight to his head.

"Mitchell, if everybody that J.C. Spivey pushed filed a suit, they would never build a courthouse big enough."

I grabbed Vicki's hand and ignored her comments about the county's personal leave time policy as I shoved her out the door towards my station wagon. "Call Purdy and tell him I've got the police station covered on this murder thing."

Last I saw in my rearview mirror as the tires sort of squealed and Vicki cried, or maybe it was the other way around, Ladawn and Mitchell were standing in the door of the Victorian Room. Ladawn was shaking her head and Mitchell was still the color of his thirty-one-point-weave oxford cloth.

Sisters. One of the great mysteries of the universe. Have a little birthday luncheon with one and go bail the other out of jail. After all, what are sisters for?

3

I took the steps leading to the police station two at a time. Behind me, I could hear Vicki's heels hitting the sidewalk in an erratic rhythm. The small wooden sign above the door read POLICE.

There has been a bit of controversy over the name of our police station. The county judge, who holds court there once a month, feels it should be called the Martinsboro Justice Building. He feels it may be unsettling for the individuals involved in the legal process to think they are walking into a police station.

Since the building also houses the municipal complex and the library, Idaleen Newsome jumped on the bandwagon and insisted they start calling it just that. She thought going to court in a building called the Martinsboro Public Library and Other Offices would have a calming effect on the criminal mind. Ed Massey, J.C.'s senior officer, said if they start calling it the library he's quitting because wasn't anybody in town going to be able to call him a sissy that worked at the library. The municipal people, being true public servants and afraid for their jobs, seemed to have no opinion at all. They, judging from past experience, will wait for an expensive sign to be erected to quote an obscure statute making the name on the sign illegal and the sign obsolete.

For the time being they are rotating the signs so that on alternate days the one-floor brick structure is called Martinsboro Police Station or Martinsboro Public Library and Other Offices, except on the one day a month they hold court. Then it is called the Martinsboro Justice Center. The maintenance supervisor for the town changes the big sign when he raises the flag in front of the building every morning. Edgar says it will take a special committee appointed by the town commissioners to solve the problem.

The committee, of course, will hire some expensive consultant to assess everyone's feelings, investigate legal options, and project a criminal's emotional response through biofeedback. Edgar says the government will use any excuse to waste money. His pet example is the time the county commissioners hired that group of consultants to increase county workers' productivity through stress relief and relaxation. Vicki said mostly what those consultants did was have them close their eyes and pretend they were butter melting into the cracks of the sidewalk. She said all in all she'd be a whole lot more relaxed if the county manager, Furman Crawford, would quit yelling until his face turned red and his veins stuck out every time things didn't go his way and, well, as long as we're on the subject, she said it would also be less stressful if he'd quit making remarks about women's behinds that were outside the bounds of fair comment.

J.C.'s way of combating the sign bureaucracy was to have Buck Faircloth take a piece of scrap lumber and fashion a sign in his spare time. The small sign hangs seven days a week above the one door that leads directly into J.C.'s area of the building. The colors were purple and yellow to reflect the chief's college football loyalties. That probably is against city code, but none of the town employees were willing to mention it to J.C.

As I came out of the entryway into the hall, the assembled officers, which to my count was the entire Martinsboro force (four excluding J.C. and including Buck the part-timer), parted as if a giant comb were being pulled through them. Only the two Department of Motor Vehicles officers that are in town on Tuesdays to issue driver's licenses held fast. These two women, being from somewhere over on the other side of the county, had no idea I was the alleged perpetrator's sister. Uniformed arms pulled them out of my way. I passed the window in the wall that had another purple-and-gold police sign hanging above it. On each side, the signs made of copier paper read WE DO NOT HAVE CHANGE FOR A DOLLAR and THIS IS NOT THE INFORMATION DESK. No use in stopping and speaking to the dispatcher, Jackie. She was in the hall with everyone else, not that I had any intention of speaking with her anyway. Ed Massey and Pete Avery had stepped back in the doorway of the office. Ed shifted slightly so the hand-lettered sign on the yellow legal pad paper could be seen. PERSONNEL ONLY was lettered in black, and, at the bottom of the paper in smaller red letters, AUTHORITY: CHIEF J.C.

SPIVEY. Ed was going to have to come up with something better than that sign to keep me from my sister.

Behind me I could hear Vicki coming down the hall. "Excuse me, beg your pardon, how are y'all doing?" Good manners are central to her life. The door to J.C.'s office was open about halfway and I headed towards it. Ed stepped in my way.

"Mrs. Upchurch, you can't go in there right now, ma'am."

I proceeded to let him know that if my sister was in that office I would be going in. In all fairness, I would give him ten seconds to get himself out of my way, and at that time it would be every man for himself—or woman, as the case may be.

"Mrs. Upchurch, they got official police business going on in there right now."

"Well, that will work out well since I'm here on official family business. Step aside."

I was positioning myself to end run him when J.C. stepped into his office doorway. Behind him I could see a pair of legs ending in high-heeled red leather cowboy boots.

J.C.'s more-than-nineteen years on the force are beginning to show. His hairline and his waistline appear to be in a race, one getting bigger, the other smaller, like two speeding trains going in opposite directions. He is Vicki's age, and I still remember him as a skinny teenager in jeans who lived to pick at and tease all of us younger children. But when it came to anybody really trying to pick on us, he would run them off in a heartbeat.

"Barbara Gail." He uses my middle name to irritate me. "Please come in. I've been expecting you."

If you have never been in J.C.'s office, you have missed a treat. The office is decorated in purple and yellow, the colors of East Carolina University. The ECU Pirates are J.C.'s favorite team. He even has an ECU bumper sticker on his special chief's car. There are several ceramic pieces and needlepoint pictures noting J.C.'s team loyalty. These are the handiwork of Eunice, J.C.'s wife. The stellar piece of ceramic work in his office is a purple-and-yellow golf ball about eight inches in diameter that sits in the middle of his credenza on its own wooden stand. Eunice does all her ceramic work over at the Ceramic Shack in Erwin. They have a kiln and everything over there. I have heard from more than several sources that Eunice does sell quite a few of those penguins with holes in their stomachs that you fill with baking soda and put in your refrigerator to keep out odors.

In the middle of all this purple and yellow sat Angel, like some tacky-red accent piece. Tears had streaked her makeup and her eyes had that puffy look that you get after you've had a good cry. She jumped up and grabbed me.

"It's the red in my karma. I tell you it's the red in my karma. Madame Zsa Zsa was right. I should have listened to her sooner."

Angel has been in quite a few scrapes over the years, but I had never seen her so upset. I patted her shoulders and comforted her for a minute before I turned back to J.C. " I suppose you think you're going to get Man of the Year or something for cleaning up the streets. Just what in heaven's name is going on here?"

"Well, Barbara Gail, we have evidence that your sister murdered Manly Richards. Based on that evidence, I am getting ready to book her and take her to

Lillington. Before she goes to the county jail over there, I've been advising her to call a lawyer. She keeps trying to call Madame Zsa Zsa. I told her if this woman had got psychic powers, no need to use her one call getting in touch with her—just send out some signals over the psychic air waves." When I didn't respond, he continued. "You need to get her to lay off this madame and get a good attorney on the phone. That's why we waited. Purdy said Mitchell had gone after you, and I figured you'd show up any minute, maybe talk some sense into her. The last thing I need is a big discombobulation when we get to Lillington."

"And just what proof do you have she killed him?"

"Her fingerprints were all over the five-pound weight that knocked him in the head."

"Really. Well, I'm sure only about half of Harnett County has fingerprints on one weight or another over at that gym. You can't arrest her for staying in shape."

"There weren't no other prints on the weight; it was completely clean except for Angel's prints."

I asked him if he thought Angel was a complete idiot. "Does it make sense to you that Angel would clean off the barbell and then put her fingerprints on it for you to find?"

"Barbara Gail, it was a crime of passion. Don't make sense to me that a grown woman needs to run her life by what someone named Madame Zsa Zsa says."

He had a point there.

"And as long as you brought it up, I can't imagine for the life of me that the beforementioned individual would dress all in red from her head to her feet because some broad who looks like she came out of an 'I Love Lucy' episode told her it would get rid of her cursed carmel or whatever the hell it is. I'm not a lawyer, but between you and me you better get her some different clothes for court."

I turned to look at Angel. She had gotten quiet and was staring intently at her lap. Her blouse was red. Her miniskirt was red. Even her stockings were red. Now her face reddened a bit.

"Angel, honey, what is he talking about?"

She sniffed a few times. Even her sniff sounded feminine. Mine always sound like some creature of the forest performing a mating call.

"I told J.C. that I went to see Madame Zsa Zsa this morning. If I'd only gone Saturday or Sunday night . . . this whole thing might have been avoided if I had only acted sooner to get this unnatural red out of my karma!"

"Angel, get a hold of yourself! I think all those chemicals you've been putting on your hair have started to seep through to your brain. This is real life we're talking about. Lord knows it's not enough that Mama and Daddy will probably need CPR when they hear the news and that Vicki is in the next room, most likely politely fainted in some corner, but you have to continue to make an idiot of yourself over this Madame Zsa Zsa who isn't anything but poo poo. She doesn't even know you see colors in people's auras, not their karmas." I'd found a book late Monday at the Dancing Stars bookshop. "You have got to snap out of this nonsense."

"Promise me you'll go see Madame Zsa Zsa. Promise." She leaned forward and clutched J.C.'s desk until her knuckles turned white. It was so unlike her to get this upset.

"Oh, I'm going to see Madame Zsa Zsa and few other people, too."

J.C. shot me a frown. I ignored him. As I turned to ask Angel a few more questions, a loud male voice came from outside the door.

"I don't understand what the holdup is." The door swung open. A man stepped into the office; he was tall and slender enough to look reedy. His suit looked as if it could use a good pressing. "Chief Spivey, what's taking so long? This woman should have been in Lillington hours ago."

His voice trailed off when he saw me. I stood behind Angel with my hand on her shoulder. "Who is she?"

Well, so much for manners.

J.C. shifted his weight back and forth. "She is Mrs. Larue's sister, Barbara Upchurch. Barbara, this is Agent Bailey from the State Bureau of Investigation. They have been helping us out with the lab work from the crime scene."

The man stared first at me, then at J.C.

"We allowed her to see Mrs. Larue because we were having trouble keeping her coherent. This isn't Raleigh, you know."

I tried to look innocent and non-threatening.

"Chief Spivey, this seems to me to be a little out of order. The suspect hasn't been booked yet."

Angel reached up and covered my hand with hers.

"Mrs. Upchurch is leaving to go call a lawyer." J.C. sounded nonchalant, but the look he gave me was pushing me to agree.

"Actually, I had a few more questions to ask my sister."

J.C.'s look became a glare. Under normal circumstances, it would be enough to make me think twice. These were hardly normal circumstances.

"If I could have two minutes to clear up a few personal

things then I'm certain I could leave you two to do your job."

The two men looked at one another.

"She can't hurt anything at this point, and she may get her a lawyer. It will make our job a hell of a lot easier."

J.C. seemed to almost plead with Agent Bailey. Agent Bailey nodded and stalked from the room, looking very much like someone had licked his candy.

"Two minutes." The door slammed behind J.C.

So there we sat, as close as two people can be and as far apart as if the Atlantic Ocean ran through J.C.'s office. I wanted to shake Angel for getting herself into this mess. And at the same time I wanted to reach out and hug her. Tears were something Angel rarely experienced, though I have to say I think she was more upset at her bad karma than her imminent arrest.

What in the world were we going to do now? It's altogether one thing to go bail her out for writing bad checks; it's quite another to look at a charge of first-degree murder. I had no idea where to start. And with only a few minutes until Frik and Frak opened the door, I needed to get moving.

Angel shifted in her chair and sniffed loudly. I knew that much as I'd like to keep lecturing, this was no time for me to get on my soapbox for moderate behavior. If she started crying again that would only slow us down, and I needed information.

Where to start? I pushed out of my mind the thought that Angel had on occasion been known to tell not just little white lies, but a virtual rainbow of them, and started trying to determine what had actually taken place.

"We don't have much time, so I want you to stick to the important parts, okay?"

She nodded and pushed back a wisp of blonde hair that had fallen across her face.

"How long have you been seeing Manly?"

I thought that was a pretty decent first question. Certainly beat "How the hell did you get mixed up in all of this," which is what I wanted to ask.

"Well, I've been working out at the Iron Body since I got back into town, so about two months I guess. I'd only started dating Manly in the last month."

I must have curled my lip, because she added, "You really had to know him, Barbara; he was a very sensitive guy. A real nineties man," before I could take a breath. Sensitive, that's exactly how I would describe Manly. A peach in the garden of love.

"I know you want to think kindly of the dead, Angel, but honestly, don't you suppose Manly played the field? Maybe somebody like Belinda Bullard?"

"Barbara, his interest in Belinda was purely professional. He told me so himself." Her voice rose a little at the end of the sentence and she glared at me. She chose to date scum of the earth, and now she was mad at me for questioning his morals.

I held up my hands with the palms towards her. "I don't care if he was seeing Marilyn Quayle. This isn't about me trying to stop you from dating the man, Angel. He's dead. What I'm trying to do here is save you from a very unpleasant experience—the rest of your life in prison, or worse. Just answer the questions."

"Fine." She crossed her arms in front of her.

"Did you know he was married?"

She rolled her eyes. "Of course I did, but he was—"

"Divorcing his wife." We spoke the last three words in unison.

"Well, Barbara, he was; he had a house over in High Cotton Estates that he was renting until the papers came through and he could buy another one."

At last, something that was useful. I hadn't heard anyone mention that he was renting a house over in High Cotton Estates, a new subdivision at the edge of town. Somehow, I couldn't picture him heading up the neighborhood watch committee.

She continued. "I know his wife's name is Bunny and she lives in a trailer north of Lillington." She recrossed her legs and adjusted her skirt. "Bunny's a silly name. He says she doesn't have a lot up here." Angel tapped the side of her head and gave me a knowing look.

"I wonder what he ever saw in her," I asked, but the sarcasm intended was lost on Angel in her present state, and maybe always. "Were you at the Iron Body Sunday night?"

At this she began to cry, and I found myself rubbing her arm as she told me about finding Manly's body.

"I worked from three to ten Sunday evening. I would have stayed until eleven, but we were so slow Martha let me go early. I called Manly around eight-thirty and we decided to have supper after I got off work. He told me he was having business meetings and not to come before ten-thirty. So I went over after I left the truck stop, and when I got there the lights were on, so I went on into the office and there he was across the desk. The barbell was beside his head, and I moved it because I wanted to touch him. He was already cold and it frightened me so bad I dropped the barbell. There was a noise out front so I ran out the side door. I was so afraid I didn't want to go home. I went to Martha's place. She gave me a key when I first came back to town. Martha didn't get in until five from the truck stop, and she finally convinced me to call the police about ten o'clock yesterday morning. Of course, by then they had already found the body."

There was no point in fussing at her about the complete lack of reasonable behavior in the scenario. What was obvious to the rest of us was not always obvious to her. I knew she was better when she said, "Be sure and let Mama and Daddy know I'm all right. Are you going to tell them about everything?" It was classic Angel to think I could keep it from them.

There was no point in fussing at her about her Johnny-come-lately sense of concern for how Mama and Daddy might take everything. This was Angel pure and simple. If this episode didn't help her psychological development catch up with her physical development, nothing would.

"Since it will most likely be on the evening news, I imagine the smart choice would be to go ahead and tell them."

I got the address of Manly's house in town, Madame Zsa Zsa's number, and general directions for finding Bunny Richards's trailer. It wasn't a huge amount of information, but at least I could get started. The door opened and J.C. walked into the office. Angel stood and I hugged her.

"Promise me if I take care of this that you won't try to contact Madame Zsa Zsa. And don't make any statements to the police until Sam Quakenbush gets there. I'm going to go call him right now."

She nodded.

J.C. guided her out to the main office with his hand

on her elbow and called for Ed. Through the open door
I saw a sobbing Vicki throw her arms around Angel who
comforted her with words I couldn't hear. As he closed
the door J.C. told Ed he'd be out in one minute.

"Barbara Gail, we have got an open-and-shut case on
this one, and I know she's your sister and all, but don't
go making it worser on all of you. Sam Quakenbush is
a good lawyer. You let him handle it."

I was wide-eyed and innocent.

"I'm serious, Barbara Gail. Like you told Angel, this
is real life. The SBI has assigned Agent Bailey to help
us process the crime scene and he won't take kindly to
some reporter messing around in things, muddying up
the waters and all, particularly and especially with you
being Angel's sister and all."

Now we were getting closer to the truth; J.C. didn't
want me to rock the boat if the SBI had a chance of
getting splashed.

"I'm only going to check on a few people who might
help Angel and work on getting her out from under
Madame Zsa Zsa's spell." I smiled contritely.

J.C. looked at me warily as he opened the door. We
walked into the main office to find Ed and Pete minis-
tering alternately to Vicki and Angel beside the file
cabinets. Agent Bailey was slumped in the dispatcher's
chair, tapping his feet nervously on the broken tile
under the chair. Jackie, the dispatcher, was holding
court in the hall with other town employees and curious bystanders. I saw Mitchell Hardison out there
with the newspaper camera.

J.C. took charge. "Okay Ed, let's ride. Pete, you stay
here and cover anything that comes in on the phone.
And get rid of all these gawkers in the hall."

Everyone moved, and I looked frantically for something to cover the lens of the *News Herald* camera with. I spotted a copy of the newspaper laying on Jackie's desk. I grabbed it and spread the pages out wide, moving to block any good shot Mitchell might have of the scene. By the time he figured out what was going on, J.C. and Ed had Angel in the chief's car. Across the parking lot, a red truck equipped with siren came roaring up and blocked the car. Out jumped Buck Faircloth. I hadn't even missed him from the station. He was smiling and waving. I momentarily forgot about Mitchell.

"Miss Angel! Miss Angel! I had to go to three stores but I finally found you a Diet Coke with no caffeine. I was tore up thinking I was going to miss you."

He looked like a school boy offering his girlfriend a present.

J.C. opened the front passenger door and got out glaring at Buck over the top of the car.

"Damnation, Buck. What the hell are you doing?"

Before Buck could reply, Agent Bailey was leaning out of his car window, twisting his neck to see what was happening.

"Chief Spivey, what is the holdup?"

"It's nothing. We're leaving right now. He's gonna get that truck out of the way. Immediately."

J.C. glared another second at Buck, who had by now made his delivery and been thanked. As the chief slid back into the car and slammed the door, Buck loped off to move his truck, whistling to himself.

Mitchell stood behind me, whining about not getting a good shot.

"Purdy is going to be really unhappy when he hears

about this, Barbara. Don't think I'm not going to tell him about you and that newspaper."

"Honestly, Mitchell, get a life."

Vicki and I returned to the dispatcher's office, where Jackie broke off a conversation with the two Department of Motor Vehicles officers in mid-sentence. She offered us the use of an empty office down the hall, where I called Sam Quakenbush. He said he'd head right over to the jail and do what he could for Angel.

I called Edgar at the mill and got his voice mail. Most of the time I like voice mail. It doesn't argue with you. It accepts whatever you say and gives you a beep in return. This time I wanted a human even if I knew he might argue with me. I pressed 0 for the plant operator and she paged him for me. I dreaded in some small way having to tell him about Angel. He was always telling me he took me for better or for worse but not for my sister.

"Hey, sweetie, listen, do you think it's possible that your mom could get the kids to the dentist this afternoon? She's on the list to pick them up at school," I said when he came on the line.

"I'll call and find out. If she's home I know she won't mind." A slight pause. "Barbara, what's going on?" There was an edge to his voice.

"Angel's got a small problem. Remember when I told you last night what Idaleen Newsome told me in the bookstore about Angel and that health club owner? Well, he was murdered last night."

"Uh-huh. And?"

"Well, J.C. has some harebrained idea that Angel murdered that man. Now I have to get Vicki on back to work; you remember today was her birthday. So I

need for you to go down to the jail and be there for the
magistrate's hearing. Sam said somebody from the
family needed to be there and, well, I've got to check
on a couple of people after I leave Vicki, and then I'll
need to go by and see what I can do for Mama and
Daddy. You don't have to go by yourself; Vicki says she
is sure Joe Dan will be happy to go with you."

"The last thing I need is Joe Dan Macauley accompa-
nying me to the magistrate's office to tend to whatever
mess it is your sister is in now."

I covered the phone while Edgar vented a bit more,
and told Vicki, "Edgar says to tell you happy birthday
and he doesn't think it's necessary for Joe Dan to go with
him. Doesn't want to worry him, with that heart problem and all." I took my hand off the phone and waited
for Edgar to pause for breath. "So I can count on you?"

He breathed heavily into the phone. "As soon as I
tell the office that I won't be back and get Jessica to
reschedule my afternoon department managers meeting, I'm on my way. Do you mind telling me who these
people are that you're going to be checking on this
afternoon?"

"I don't know their names myself. No use worrying
Edgar with details. "But I'll tell you all about it
tonight." Thank your mama for me and order pizza if
you get home before I do. I love you."

I called Aunt Louise to go break the news to Mama
and Daddy; I was afraid that by the time I got Vicki
back to work somebody would have already called and
told them. And if I took Vicki by to help me tell them,
well, that would be the afternoon right there. There
was too much to be done to figure this thing out. Also,
I'm generally chicken when it comes to being the

bearer of bad news for my parents, though I should be a professional at it by now. Angel's problems typically left my parents discouraged. And they were surprised, too, as if she normally lived the life of a minister's wife instead of her sort of free-spirited lifestyle.

I hustled Vicki out to the car and tried to decide who would have the most information that could help Angel.

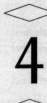

4

By the time we reached the station wagon, Vicki had gotten her face together and was working on her emotions. First things first. She needed to get her car and go by the office. I needed to go by the *News Herald* and talk to Purdy. While I was there I could check on exactly who owned the Iron Body Health Club. I dropped her in front of the courthouse in Lillington and was at the newspaper office in fifteen minutes.

The offices of the *Martinsboro News Herald* were quiet for a Tuesday. Tuesday was our deadline day, but with the Thanksgiving holiday on Thursday, our usual publication day, the deadline had been moved to Monday. The rush was over for the week.

I made my way to my office through stacks of sale flyers destined to be inserted in the paper. My "office" is one of four computer stations built into a room in the back. The other three stations belong to Mitchell

Hardison, Jay Cannaday, and Velena Moore. Mitchell and Jay cover the wrecks in town, local trials, fires, and other happening things. They consider these events glamorous journalism. I cover schools, town board and county commissioners, social events, and anything someone else isn't available to cover.

Velena Moore writes the church notes and the religious column. Her column has a little picture of her right at the top next to the title, "Velena's Views." If someone relied on that picture to pick her out of a crowd, they probably wouldn't recognize her. She insists the paper use a picture that's twenty-five years old. Velena likes to have us close our eyes and visualize our needs being met. She is certain prosperity can be achieved through prayer and visualization. (Until it gets here, she is driving a 1970 Falcon.)

The half of the office that Mitchell and Velena occupy has neat piles of paper and desk sets beside the computer equipped with scissors, tape, and all the important things you need to write a story. The half of the office Jay and I occupy looks ninety percent of the time like a bomb has been dropped on it. Papers seem to have a life of their own, moving from one spot to another and occasionally mating with the help of the Diet Mountain Dew I drink or the coffee Jay keeps on his desk. (Sometimes until green things form around the edge of his coffee cup. Diet Mountain Dew doesn't grow green things—too many chemicals in it.) I keep a house clean enough to function around five people's lives; the office is the last refuge of my masculine side.

In search of a legal pad, I plowed through several phone books, a listing of all the school principals and the school board members in the county, a bottle of aspirin, and three versions of a story I wrote two weeks ago. I found one under a *Town of Martinsboro Code of Ordinances* book that someone had left on my desk. (Jay and I agree that Mitchell tidies up his work station by throwing all the extraneous stuff into our area.) Grabbing the pad, I made my way to the file room in the back. I began going through the file cabinets in search of anything I could find on the Iron Body Health Club. There was only one article. It bore Jay's byline and was a feature on the grand opening, complete with a picture of Manly Richards smiling with his arms around several women in leotards. I backtracked to the office.

In contrast to Mitchell's snooty ways and bottles of mineral water, Jay is real down to earth and easygoing. A touch on the naïve side, though; last year he actually believed that advertisement titled "Scientists Make Amazing Discovery Regarding Hair Growth." He has a round look, sort of like the Pillsbury Dough Boy with clothes and brown hair.

When I showed him the Iron Body article, he remembered Manly telling him that there were other investors, but they wanted to be silent partners. In fact, Manly hadn't even mentioned their names.

"Barbara, I think Purdy was looking for you." Jay was staring at the floor.

"He most certainly is. I told him all about the police station," Mitchell said. He came marching in with his nose elevated. I shot him what my children call *the look*. His nose dropped half an inch. "Well, Barbara, I had to tell him something since I didn't get a decent picture. I mean Buck Faircloth presenting the murder suspect with the soft drink of her choice is hardly front-page stuff. And now all the cameras are missing. I suppose you don't know anything about that?"

My look remained unchanged.

"You should know better. After all, you are a lot older than the rest of the reporting staff." Mitchell loved to throw up the fact that I was older, like somehow being over thirty made me age-impaired.

"Mitchell, I've got more than cameras on my mind. You can't keep up with your stuff, that's not my problem. All my children outgrew the colic at about twelve weeks. I didn't realize it could last until you're twenty-two years old."

I walked off in search of Purdy, whose office is in the very front of the building. The staff parked in the back, so I hadn't been by his office yet. The central hall in the *News Herald* office is formed by wood veneer partitions that end about three-quarters of the way up to the ceiling. The partitions' top third is made of Plexiglas. Behind these little shields, people got very involved in their tasks as I walked through. Only Alice, who is Purdy's administrative assistant and the informal assignment editor, met my eyes.

Alice and I had come to the *Martinsboro News Herald* from very different directions, but had formed a fast friendship. It evolved out of, among other things, our love of gospel music, actually black gospel music. We discovered this quite by accident.

I had been in the office trying to get tickets to see James Taylor at the Dean Dome, calling off and on all day. I banged the phone down after listening to a busy signal for what seemed like the hundredth time. Alice walked in looking for a picture we were going to run about the time Jay said, "Can't get James Taylor, huh?"

"If you can't get him, Barbara, I know his first cousin Maurice. He's at Maurice's a lot. You could call and leave a message for him."

I turned around in my chair. "Alice, I'm talking about the James Taylor."

"So am I, child. The one that makes that barbecue sauce everyone's crazy over."

"Right. Does he sing 'Fire and Rain' and 'Carolina in My Mind'?"

Alice stopped searching through the pile of pictures. "Doesn't sing at all that I know about."

At that point I half hummed, half sang my entire James Taylor repertoire, with Jay doing backup. She'd never heard one of them.

"I can't believe you don't know James Taylor."

"Oh, really." She gave me a look I couldn't quite read. "I suppose you know Heavy D. and the Boyz or Ice Cube?"

"No."

"How about Mary J. Blige and her song, 'What's the 411'?" She crossed her arms in front of her.

I shook my head, laughing at myself.

She named off three more singers I'd never heard of, a hint of a smile on her face.

I was laughing. "I'm starting to feel middle-class white."

Now she laughed. "Child, you *are* middle-class white."

We were both laughing now. Jay looked confused; he obviously couldn't decide whether to laugh or not. I tried to think of names. The Supremes, Aretha Franklin. Too easy. Andrae Crouch. "Andrae Crouch." Andrae Crouch was one of the first musicians to

bridge that gap between black gospel music and the
white church.

She caught her breath and wiped her eyes. "You listen to Andrae Crouch?"

I nodded.

"There is hope yet," she said.

Shortly after that, Alice had tickets to a gospel concert at Memorial Auditorium. She invited me along. It
was that night that marked a turning point in our friendship. Alice told me on the way home about singing the
words over and over to "I've Got Confidence" as her
husband beat her. He'd gotten violently high off something and she was afraid she was going to die. She had
pulled herself into the bathroom and locked the door,
looking for anything to hit him with should he go after
the children, Jameel and Kecia, who were asleep in
the next room. He had gone off to find more liquor
and she had sung to herself as she bundled the children, their bodies limp with sleep, into the car. "I
thought I was going to die that night. The words to
that song played over and over in my mind—to keep
me going, I guess," she said. She never looked back.
Three years after her divorce, she had met and married Reginald, a computer programmer for IBM.

We talked on the way home about growing up. Alice
was sent out at ten years of age to iron for well-to-do
white families, raising the other children in her family
so her mother could work. My own childhood had
been so different, but we found common ground, first
in the music, then in children, sexism, gripes with
spouses, relationships with families, all the things
where women find common ground.

Alice can do three to five things at once. I've seen

her work out a scheduling problem for Purdy, figure out a story assignment, locate a back article for the mayor's office, and help me decide my best course of action when Jason's second-grade teacher said he was a slow learner.

Alice stood in front of me now, looking more twenty than almost forty. She put her hand on my arm. "I don't know who killed him, girl, but I know they are going to be one sorry soul your sister ever got accused of doing it. I've seen that look on your face." Her hand was patting my arm. "I'll do anything I can to help you make it right."

I smiled at her and tears came to my eyes. Sometimes kindness has a way of bringing out what nothing else can. The task before me looked monumental, and Alice was one of those friends who offered to help and meant it.

"Now look, girl." She squeezed my arm and her eyes held a message. "The cameras seem to have been misplaced. Even the one Mitchell was using is gone. I don't know how long they're gonna be out of circulation. Long enough, I guess, for Mitchell to lose interest and keep Angel's picture out of the paper next week. By then, I'm counting on you to have this thing solved."

That's what Mitchell meant earlier. I smiled and wiped my eyes. I entered Purdy's office with a firm step. He came around from behind the desk and offered one of the chairs with his hand.

He's kind of short for a man, only around 5'5", a little taller depending on what shoes he has on. I'm a good three inches taller than he is when I wear heels. I wear heels when we fight about stories. I wonder if that is how Josephine dealt with Napoleon. Purdy's dark hair is graying somewhat. He is a benign Republican, if there is such a thing. While the editorials in the paper definitely reflect his conservative tendencies, he is bipartisan when he goes after any corruption in government or injustice to human nature.

"Barbara Gail, you know if there is anything we can do, all you have to do is ask. How are your mama and daddy doing?"

"I don't know. I'm going to stop by there on my way home. Purdy, you know she didn't do it."

He took off his glasses and ran his hand down his face. "You understand, we're going to have to run the stories. If we don't we'll compromise our journalistic integrity." "Journalistic integrity" is Purdy's favorite phrase. He uses it to impress the local civic organizations and book clubs when he is called upon to speak.

"I understand, Purdy. Just try to hold off from too much detail until I can get some more information together so J.C. will go sniff up some other tree."

"I'll do what I can. Do you need some time off?"

"I think I'm okay."

I didn't have that much on the calendar for the next few weeks and I could count on Jay to help me in a pinch.

"Good, because if this settles down in time, I'm counting on you for a good human interest piece on this year's Christmas parade." Things were back to normal as far as Purdy was concerned.

The Christmas parade. I made one more mental note to call Ladawn Pittman about recruiting Alice to help in my place and got up to go finish my research.

"Purdy, do you remember any mention of the partners in the Iron Body Health Club?"

He paused to think, massaging his temples as if that

would help. "I can't recall anyone being mentioned other than this Richards character."

I moved towards the door. The police scanner in the hall went off, giving out information on the location of a wreck. Out of habit, Purdy and I both stopped to listen.

"One more thing, Barbara Gail, tell Alice to look in her drawer for one of the cameras. Jay is going to need it to cover that wreck. We'll use a file photo of the Iron Body building with this murder story."

As he rubbed his hand back down his face, I could see he was smiling.

I hurried out, pausing long enough to give Alice the scoop on the camera. I hadn't thought Manly's partners would be so mysterious. I was irritated at the trouble it was to find them.

There was so much to do. I called the funeral home and got more specific directions to the trailer where Manly's wife lived as well as a phone number. I called and was greeted by a nasal voice which identified itself as Bunny Richards. She was completely indisposed all afternoon and evening, but could squeeze in a morning appointment. By the time I checked on the results of Angel's bail hearing and made sure Mama and Daddy were okay, the day would be pretty well shot anyway. It was awful to have to talk with her so soon after Manly's death, but what choice did I have in this whole thing? I called Vicki, who had regained her composure and insisted on going with me to talk with Bunny.

"I'm not going to let you go alone and that's final. Who knows anything about this woman? She could be a criminal sort just like her husband. Birds of a feather—"

"Okay, Vicki. I'll pick you up at ten. It'll be nice to have company."

Not really. But what good would it do to hurt Vicki's feelings at this point? One of the things Dad would say to us when we had throw downs over attendance at a family function was, "You're going to go, you're going to have fun, and you're going to say you had fun." I find myself saying something similar to Becky these days. Becky is our oldest child. Without a doubt, she has shown Edgar and I that life doesn't really begin until you have a thirteen-year-old.

"I only hope she knows the names of the health club partners," I added.

I had to admit I was curious as well as anxious about meeting the woman who was married to Manly Richards. Maybe she had the answers that Angel needed.

5

The black-and-white trailer was a double-wide. The best money could buy. Out front was parked the shiniest Trans Am you have ever seen. The color was that new green that's so popular, not quite aqua, more like teal. The license plate read, BUNNY.

Mrs. Bunny Richards was no surprise. When she opened the front door for Vicki and me on Wednesday, she was smoking, one of those thin brown cigarettes that looks like it wants to grow up to be a cigar. She bore a strange resemblance to the captain of Oklahoma Red Heat, a roller derby team I've seen on TV when I go over to the Upchurches's. Mrs. Upchurch likes to watch the Roller Derby; her favorite teams are Oklahoma Red Heat and Mississippi Mud Marauders.

Bunny Richards ground out her cigarette and popped a piece of chewing gum into her mouth. She sat on her black-velour couch smacking her chewing gum and smirking at us as we sat in matching black-velour chairs. The kitchen, which we could see across a white countertop adorned with several cigarette cartons, was devoid of any of the usual appointments of a death in the household. Not one chicken casserole, not one bowl of potato salad, not even a bucket of Kentucky Fried Chicken or a deli tray from the Winn Dixie could be seen. It was evident from the counter that Bunny Richards did not have any close friends, belong to a church, or bowl in a league. No self-respecting organization in Martinsboro and the surrounding communities would allow one of its members to grieve without dinner. Our community still meets death through the most vital organ, the stomach. Food is sometimes the only comfort you can give.

Bunny Richards did not look like a member of the Ladies' Auxiliary. Her face had the texture of a fruit roll-up, those dried-up snacks that the children eat. She wore heavy make up and an orange shade of eyeshadow that I had no idea existed. The blonde in her hair expired about four inches from the top of her head, so that a nondescript shade of brown came through. The orange sweater she was wearing was tight across a chest that gave the appearance of coming straight out of Dolly Parton's gene pool. Her jeans were so tight that I had been amazed that she was able to bend enough to sit instead of having to lean back and sort of fall like the model in a hypnotist's experiment.

Vicki kept smiling at no one in particular and smoothing her skirt; if she continued at that rate she would wear a hole right through that knit dress of hers. Meanwhile, I was deciding which way to begin the discussion. We had gotten past expressions of sympathy and the conversation was at an awkward standstill. It

was a rather delicate undertaking, and I am much better at your straightforward, bulldozer kind of conversation than I am your let's-fly-all-around-it and
light-gently-upon-it-like-fairies variety. I had ruled
out, for reasons of tact and personal safety, "Mrs.
Richards, we are here because our sister Angel was
messing around with your husband," and I was sort of
favoring, "Mrs. Richards, are you aware that your husband and our sister Angel were special friends?" Then
it came to me I should start out with something general and non-threatening like, "Mrs. Richards, it is
unfortunate that morals in America are deteriorating
at an alarming rate."

Before I could begin, she popped her chewing gum
twice in a row and said, "Ain't it funny how women
with nicknames appealed to Manly? Names like mine,
Bunny, or your sister's name, Angel. Course, names like
Melissa, Jane, Rita, Belinda, Emily, Renee, Deborah,
Becky, Valerie, Paula—well, you get the picture, all
kinds of names appealed to Manly. I gave up a long
time ago trying to keep up with them." Each name was
punctuated with a pop of her chewing gum. "The
police have already questioned me about every woman
in town. I'll tell you like I told them, I gave up fighting
with Manly over women years ago. I don't know nothing about any of his local lovehoneys."

"Well, Mrs. Richards, maybe you could just tell us a
little bit about yourself and Mr. Richards. As you
know, our sister Angel has been arrested for his murder, and we would really appreciate any information
you could give us."

"Call me Bunny. Really, there ain't much to tell. I
met Manly ten years ago when he was judging a bikini

contest I entered in Myrtle Beach. It was love at first
sight and I thought I'd won the grand prize when he
asked me out afterwards. Shortly after, we started dating, and as soon as he found out that my pop had just
died and left me his brownstone in Brooklyn, he
wanted to tie the knot. We weren't married six weeks
when he convinced me to sign it all over to him for
'investment.' I was too stupid to see which way the
wind blew until the money was all gone."

The bitterness in her voice made me shake my head
in sympathetic response, and Vicki stopped her skirt
smoothing long enough to say, "Well, bless your
heart."

"It's been one health club after another since then.
He always finds some sucker to give him the money
and we leave town after dark when things don't work
out."

"So things were going badly here in Martinsboro? I
understand you two had been fighting recently."

"We fought recently and not so recently, sweetie. As
for the club, hell, this is the first time it worked. He had
money all the time; no bill collectors calling. I got the
new car out front and was working on saving enough
out of what he gave me to get back to Myrtle Beach and
live for a while before I had to find a job. Manly could
always find a sucker to float him for a while, but this
time it looked like it was really going well." She stopped
chewing and folded her hands in her lap. "I wanted to
think about having kids and all that, but he won't really
interested. When we were married, I didn't think about
it so much. When I mentioned it to him last year, he just
laughed." She began to chew again. "He was changing,
though. He would always threaten to knock me

around before when things got bad. Lately when we would fight he *really* did knock me around. Put his fist right through the bedroom wall. I threw the coffee pot at him and totaled it. That's how come I bought the gun. I figured if it was going to be him or me, it was going to be him."

I guess she'd chewed the flavor out of her gum because she spit it out into the wrapper and lit another cigarette. She waved it around as she talked. "And he was real moody; up or really down and not interested in fooling around. I could always count on him getting all hot and bothered when he came home no matter how many women he messed around with, but not lately. It was just as well; by that time I had some other interests."

Vicki was paying close attention to her hand as it smoothed her dress, and her face was red.

Bunny took note of her face and said, "Gardening, I took up gardening."

The garden of love, I was sure. "Were you and Manly separated?"

"We both did our own thing, you understand, but it wasn't anything official."

"Did you know he'd rented a house in High Cotton Estates?"

That news seemed to startle her a bit. I couldn't decide if it was because she didn't know about the house or if she was surprised because I did.

"No, I had no idea."

I asked Bunny, as she insisted I call her, a few more questions, but it seemed she knew nothing of Manly's business partners and less of his financial affairs. She could name off a half-dozen people who could have killed him, including herself, but didn't think any of them were in the area.

"Nothing personal, but did you kill your husband?"

"No, but I'm sure not sorry he's dead. I figured out a long time ago that the grand prize I won was actually the booby prize. I'll put him in the ground, but the only tears I'll cry will be if the insurance policy doesn't pay."

We left the grieving widow.

Vicki was looking a little pale as we drove towards Lillington. Working in the county manager's office was a walk in the park compared to the life of an investigative reporter. I knew she was concerned as much about how Angel got into this mess with a married man as she was about Angel having been arrested for murder.

"Vicki, we can't sweat the small stuff now. Angel's less-than-exemplary conduct is water under the bridge at this point. Our main concern is to figure out who killed Manly and get her out of jail."

Vicki let out a large sigh. I tried to cheer her.

"I know how you feel, but we'll have to wait until later to worry about Angel's other issues. Not that it will do much good; she's always done what she wants to."

I looked across the front seat of the car and thought Vicki's eyes looked a little watery. If I could get her back to work, that would take her mind off things. I asked her if she had an update on the Misty Lynn–Joshua Merriwether proposed romance.

"Nothing; I hardly talked to her at all last night with all this mess. You don't think her aunt being jailed for murder will hurt her chances, do you?"

Poor Misty Jane. The least of her problems was her relatives' unbecoming social conduct and skirmishes

with the law. Out of the corner of my eye, I saw Vicki
pull a tissue from her purse.

"I'm sure it won't make one bit of difference and I
think you've done enough for one day. The office is
probably a mess by now. Besides, you can't use up all
your vacation time on this."

Vicki put up a small protest, but I assured her I
would call her with any new developments in the case.
Her shoulders dropped a bit. "If you're sure you'll be
okay alone."

"I'll be fine. I'll use my press pass if I run into any
trouble. People respect the media." Only a small exaggeration, but necessary. I dropped her at the door of
the courthouse and hurried off to the Iron Body
Health Club.

The Iron Body Health Club was a rectangular prefab
building off the Coats highway at the edge of
Martinsboro. The back of the building faced Otis
Turlington's farm. Otis is getting on in years, and so his
son Otis Jr., who graduated with me from Martinsboro
High School, runs the farm now. They grow mostly
tobacco, I believe.

As I opened the front door of the spa, the air around
me filled with music with a pulsating beat far from the
beach music that Edgar and I love to shag to. Actually,
Edgar just shuffles his feet now and then. Between
you and me, he dances much more like Glen
Campbell than he does Elvis. He might pass for Elvis
now, since The King's been dead so long.

I shouted hello to the young man folding towels
behind the front desk. His red golf shirt had the words

Iron Body Health Club in a crescent shape on the pocket with Staff in big letters underneath. He had on a white plastic name plate with Peter York, Assistant Manager written on it in red letters.

"You here about the prenatal class?"

Without thinking, I looked at my stomach underneath the long pink sweater I was wearing. I had overindulged a bit the last few weeks. Maybe these knit stirrup pants weren't such a good idea.

"Heavens no. I'm Barbara Upchurch, and I'd like to ask you a few questions."

"About what?"

"About Manly Richards and his partners."

He snapped another towel as he folded it. "I've already told the police everything. Besides, Tracey didn't show for her morning shift on the desk and I've got to answer the phone and give out towels until Brent gets here."

"That's okay, I can stand right here and ask you everything I need to know." I plowed right on, not giving him another chance to object.

"Do you know any of the other partners in the Iron Body?"

"Nada, not a one."

"That's pretty amazing considering your position and everything."

"It's not exactly, since I make it a point to stay out of other people's business."

I ignored the remark.

"Ever meet Bunny, Manly's wife?"

Business was one thing, wives were another. "I never actually met her, but I talked to her a few times and, let me tell you, she was one hard-nosed bit—lady.

She would call up here threatening me 'cause I couldn't tell her his itinerary for the day. Like I was some social secretary. The woman is one brick short of a load; elevator doesn't go to the top, you know what I mean?"

All this from a woman who said she didn't care a bit what the man did.

"Manly said she told him she'd get him in divorce court. Said when she finished parading women through court, he wouldn't walk out with the shoes on his feet."

As far as he was concerned we had listed all the possibilities. He didn't know anyone who might have done it.

"Did you ever meet my sister?"

"Your sister?" He looked confused.

"Yes, my sister is Angel Larue."

At the mention of Angel's name, he let out a noise like the "Wheel of Fortune" crowd does when Johnny announces one of the fabulous prizes. He started to say something, seemed to catch himself, and then sort of squinted his eyes at me. "You're Angel Larue's sister?"

I resisted the urge to push the pile of towels he was folding onto the floor and smiled. "Just picture me as a blonde."

"Man, I'm sorry she was arrested. What a crock, them thinking she did it. She's one of my favorite regulars, Angel is. A real looker, too."

I threw my hand up in the air. "Runs in the family."

He had no further thoughts on potential murder candidates and wouldn't give out any information on club members. Professional ethics.

I tried again. "Who discovered the body?"

"Me. I switched shifts with Tracey, which was a real piece of luck. She would have really freaked if she'd seen him lying across the desk."

The club was closed Monday and Tuesday. Tuesday morning, he received a call from a Mr. Norman, who ran a management company in Raleigh. Mr. Norman had been hired by the partners to oversee the operation of the club, keeping Peter on to manage the day-to-day operations. The club had reopened Wednesday morning.

"I ran the place anyway, since Manly was so busy with other things."

I assumed he meant women like my sister. "What things?"

Peter's mouth clamped down as if he realized he had said more than he wanted. He glanced around and said, "Look, I've got other work to do."

I requested a peek at Manly's office. He told me it was off limits to everyone but police, under Mr. Norman's direct order. I'd have to figure out a different way to see what was in there. He was starting to drum his fingers on the top of the display case that made up the counter that was between us. I held up a finger.

"Last thing, I need to talk to Belinda Bullard. Do you know where I can find her?"

He jerked his thumb over to the left, the direction the music was coming from. I walked toward a wall of windows, past various machines resembling medieval torture racks. The place was empty at that time of the day except for a few weight lifters and a small group of lunchtime aerobic enthusiasts whom I could see through the glass. At the front of the class was a woman clad in the next-to-nothingest excuse for clothes imaginable. Her top was a bra made out of black spandex and her bottom was these little short pants of shimmery Lycra in cobalt blue and overlaid with a spandex diaper of black with no back, just a string running between the cheeks of her behind. "Butt floss," Angel calls it. She had masses of gold chains hanging from her neck and earrings that dangled and shook every time she moved. I suppose that was for some sort of athletic symmetry, since everything else was either dangling or shaking. Her hair was almost white it was so blonde and she had it pulled up and sticking out to the side.

"That's it, y'all. Have a great day. I'm gonna be checking to see if y'all are all here tomorrow for the Abs Blaster class," she said.

As the class drifted away, the instructor turned to fiddle with the stereo system. I sucked in my stomach and walked across the carpeted floor. The mirrored room reflected back to me my face furrowed in an effort not to breathe.

Glancing up from the stereo, the instructor saw my reflection and turned to greet me. Her face said, "I'm older than my body will admit to" before she even opened her mouth.

"Hi. Were you here observing class? It's a great time to start a personal fitness program." Her voice was breathy and rushed, like she was practicing to do a 900-number commercial.

I shook my head and extended my hand at the same time. "I'm Barbara Upchurch. I am a reporter for the the *Martinsboro News Herald*."

Her smile faded and her hand, which was swinging up to meet mine, dropped to her side. "I don't have anything to say. I've already spoken to the cops, in fact, to several cops."

"Now, Ms. Bullard, don't get yourself all worked up. You'll waste all those endorphins you just cooked up. It's a few little background questions on your boss, your newly departed boss." I used my most disarming smile, the one I used when Jason's kindergarten teacher got upset because he'd had a little bathroom accident. He'd peed on someone else's pants. (The little boy had extra clothes anyway.)

The stiff pose she had adopted softened somewhat.

"How long have you known Manly Richards?"

She fiddled with an earring. "Like I told the police, I met him about a year ago at the Longbranch." The Longbranch is a popular nightclub in Raleigh. "I told him I taught some at one of the gyms in Raleigh and he gave me a free pass to come work out. I live in Angier, so this was much closer, and three weeks later I was teaching two step aerobic classes for him."

"You like teaching, then?"

"Sure. A month later I was promoted to aerobics director."

"That was a pretty quick promotion."

"This is a health club, not the government; people are in and out of here so fast they should have put a revolving door out front. This business has a high turnover. Some weeks I teach more classes than I want to because we lose so many instructors with no notice."

"So you're certain that your new title didn't have anything to do with your personal relationship with Manly Richards? I have several reliable sources that say it did."

"Who said that? They're busted, because if everyone Manly Richards slept with was named aerobics director, we have one for every hour of the day and then some."

Her head was moving up and down. The side pony-tail flopped all around. The mirror close behind her doubled the movement, making me feel a little motion sick.

"I did sleep with Manly for a while, but I soon found out which way the wind blew, if you get what I'm saying. Manly had a very short attention span. My kid's teacher says he's got the same thing, only she calls it attention deficit disorder. He can't pay attention to one thing if he has any distractions at all. That's just how Manly was about women, constantly distracted by someone else. They got my kid on medicine, but I don't think they make anything to control what Manly had." The ponytail flopped on. "I got my job here because of my skill, my professional skill, that is. I'm certified by IDEA, AFFA, and ETA. I got more letters behind my name than the alphabet. I'm a trained professional and anyone who tells you different is lying."

"Do you know of anyone who did not care for Mr. Richards?"

"Honey, you don't have enough room in your paper for the list. Oh, sure, to his face everyone around here was his buddy, but behind his back, pfft, very few people liked him. Especially lately, he was the moodiest SOB you ever saw. He'd just start screaming at people over the littlest things."

Funny Tight Lips at the front desk hadn't mentioned these things.

"From one professional to another, I mean strictly off the record, why was he so moody? Was business bad? His wife threatening him? What?"

"He was in training with some of the guys for Mr. Piedmont. It was a qualifying round for the Mr. North

Carolina Muscle Mania contest, following special diets, all kinds of stuff. Personally, the last person I want to be around in this universe is some big muscle man on a limited diet. Geez, it's awful."

"So he got upset cause he lost?"

"Contest isn't even for another two weeks. No way all those muscles came from nutritional supplements, know what I mean?" Her hair flipped as her eyes scanned the room for anyone close enough to hear. "They were juicing."

I felt confused. Juice? I opened my mouth to speak.

The ponytail leaned in a little closer. "Steroids. They were using steroids to get big."

No wonder Tight Lips at the front desk wasn't talking. "Where did they get the steroids?"

"Beats me, but if I really wanted to know, I'd ask Bubba Pittman."

6

I spent the drive back to the house trying to imagine how Bubba Pittman was involved in all of this. I didn't know him all that well, but I knew how hard Ladawn had worked after her divorce to make sure he was raised right. So how much should I say to Ladawn? That was a good question. It wouldn't be in anybody's best interest to tell her what I'd heard. Maybe Belinda Bullard didn't really know what she was talking about.

Then again, maybe she did.

I'd certainly hate it if what was good for Angel turned out to be bad for Ladawn's Bubba. I hate to deceive people (okay, some people), but family's family, even if Angel was pushing the point. I wondered if what I was going to say to Ladawn qualified as a sin of omission since I planned to omit details, or a sin of commission, since I was actively telling a falsehood. I convinced myself it was on a special list and didn't qualify as a sin at all.

At the house, I realized how hungry I was from thinking about all that exercise. I made myself a peanut butter and banana sandwich, a throwback to my childhood. Peanut butter and banana sandwiches and those Little Debbie cakes with the white icing outside that have coconut sprinkled on the top and white creme in the middle are a source of comfort to me. They call it dysfunctional now if you seek comfort in food; it's much better for you to pay a psychiatrist tons of money than to pop a sugar high every now and then. When they make psychiatrists available for 99 cents in aisle five of the Food Lion, I'll think about it.

Rummaging through my purse, I came up with the number that Angel had given me for Madame Zsa Zsa. On the third ring a voice that sounded like Vincent Price's grandmother's answered. I explained who I was.

"Oh, yes, poor Angel. She was distraught Monday evening and then I saw her on the evening news."

"It is important that I see you as quickly as possible. I could come out later today, or even tomorrow after Thanksgiving lunch."

"I'm so sorry, but I'm leaving in the next hour and won't return until late tomorrow night."

"Well, Friday morning then. First thing." I felt a bit uneasy. "You aren't leaving the state or anything, are you?"

"Do not worry my dear, I'm only off to Fayetteville to enjoy a holiday meal with old friends."

I resisted the temptation to ask if they were living or dead. "Okay then, eight A.M. Friday."

The madame gave me directions and I hung up.

I stopped by the Victorian Room and pulled Ladawn aside from the dwindling lunch crowd. Her hair was pulled back in its customary knot, efficient but stylish. The silver earrings and necklace she was wearing seemed the perfect touch for the gray-and-pink jacket and pink pleated skirt she was wearing. On anyone else the combination would have looked silly.

When we were out of earshot of the late diners, she hugged me.

"I'm so sorry about Angel. Anything that I can do for you or your family, please just let me know."

"Well, I was thinking you might want Alice to take over some of my Christmas parade duties—"

Ladawn clasped her hands together. "Don't you even think of the Christmas parade. I can handle that."

I took a deep breath. "Ladawn, do you know where I might find Bubba to talk to him? I need a little background for the story on Manly Richards. I know he's a regular at the spa."

Her voice expressed her outrage. "Don't tell me Purdy Newsome is making you write stories about your own sister!"

"Not exactly; I'm helping Mitchell with a little background, that's all." That wasn't too bad. I'm sure I would give Mitchell some help with background.

"Bubba is probably at the high school using the track. I can have him call you."

"Oh, no, I'll catch up with him." I turned to go. "And Ladawn, don't let Viola Martin nominate Philip to be Santa Claus again this year. I know he's her husband, but he is too skinny to play Santa Claus. Last year, after the parade, Melissa asked me if Santa Claus was going to die."

She smiled and shook her head as I turned to go.

I drove to the high school and approached the lone

figure on the track. Bubba Pittman was a blond-haired, blue-eyed Adonis. I knew from Ladawn that he was a religious member of the Iron Body Health Club. The few times I had seen him around town lately the fabric in his shirt barely contained the muscles underneath. He had that air about him of a man used to receiving notes from strange women at restaurants. On one occasion, they say, he was visiting one of his girlfriends in Greensboro and a whole group of women broke into applause when he entered the church sanctuary, of all places. I know plenty of congregations that wouldn't applaud if Jesus himself showed up in the sanctuary. Bubba's looks are so striking because he is muscular, handsome, and pretty all at the same time. Once you talk with him, the spell is broken. In the great accounting book of life, Bubba's looks are his assets, and his brains are definitely his liabilities.

We exchanged pleasant greetings and I explained that I wanted a little information on Manly Richards and the Iron Body Health Club. "Bubba, I need to know if you know anything at all about this contraband floating around at the Iron Body."

"No ma'am, but I can tell you for a fact the Iron Body never engaged in politics and I don't think Manly had even heard of Nicaragua." He said all this to me in the same tone I use with Granny B. over at the nursing home.

"Bubba, I want to know about steroids. Illegal drug use over at the Iron Body."

The edges of his smile wavered. "I don't know about any drug use over at the Iron Body, Mrs. Upchurch, ma'am."

If he thought adding ma'am on the end of his sentence

was impressing me, he had another thing coming. "Bubba, I don't mean to be hard to get along with, but I have several sources who say you know what's going on."

"I'm shocked."

Now I was mad. He didn't realize who he was dealing with. Any woman with three kids at home could spot his con a mile away. "Be prepared for an even bigger shock. With my press connections and everything, I could ruin your career. Now, I think a lot of your mama and so I wouldn't be real happy about it. However, if it's a matter of Angel spending her life rotting in jail or you getting to prance around some football field hitting other men on the behind, I'd say my choice is clear."

He looked at me and I knew he could tell I was past the age of swooning. I was no college-age cutie that could be won over with a smile and a tweak on the cheek. That really took out his arsenal. The process of weighing alternatives played across his face like a silent picture. "Now that you mention it, I do seem to remember something about steroids over at the spa."

With a little prodding by me that consisted of repeatedly mentioning his mother's name, he admitted that he knew Manly sold steroids. He might have even bought some. Manly told him he had a great supplier who got a good cut of the deal. Manly was hiking up prices on his end and increasing his take without the supplier knowing. You had to hand it to Manly, he was consistent. He cheated everybody.

A look at my watch told me it was almost time to get the children at day care. Making Bubba promise he would call me if he remembered anything important, I drove off figuring if I were to hurry, I might be able to get some sort of response from J.C. with my news. I swung by the police station, trying to imagine J.C.'s face when I told him Manly Richards was dealing in steroids. The steroid dealing opened up many roads that could lead to murder suspects other than Angel. I was rehearsing the right tone in my voice for a pointed comment on innocent people getting hurt when people go off on these wild tangents with no proof as I parked the car and strode up the walk.

Inside, I realized that I would have to save my performance for another day. J.C. wasn't there. Behind the black metal desk where the dispatcher normally sits was the new man, Wiley Bass. He had been on the force about six months. Martinsboro was growing, and the town board had funded a new position about seven months earlier. Wiley's family was from Goldsboro, so I didn't know much about him. Being the newest officer on the force, he frequently got drafted for desk duty when Jackie was off.

His big frame stuck out at all angles from behind the desk, and he sort of unfolded when he needed to get up and move around. He leaned towards a "Terminator" look, with his close-cropped hair and mirrored sunglasses. Wiley sat up and tried to look busy when I rounded the corner past the AUTHORIZED PERSONNEL ONLY sign. He shoved a magazine into the drawer, but not before I saw the word *Muscling*, with two well developed bodies underneath it, flash by on its way underneath a stack of papers.

"J.C. is out getting ready to bag the big one, Mrs. Upchurch." He sighted an imaginary deer through the end of his finger. "He was in all morning, but he won't be back to work now until after turkey day."

I hadn't thought about deer season, I was so caught

up in helping Angel. Edgar had been airing out his clothes on the deck for a couple days now, trying to get the human scent out of them. He'd washed them in Sport Scent to take away the odor of civilization. Thanksgiving is traditionally a big day for hunters. I imagine the deer would just as soon skip it.

"Is there something I can help you with, Mrs. Upchurch? Not to be nosey or anything, but if it's about Mrs. Larue's case I am well informed about all the pertinent data and everything. Not to brag or anything, but I think the chief has taken a real liking to me. And don't worry, Mrs. Upchurch, you can tell me anything. My lips are sealed."

He was an obvious graduate of Milton Williams's course, "City Employees and the Public." That's what happens when you spend your Tuesday nights at North Carolina State University getting a master's in public administration; you come up with all kinds of ideas on making government user-friendly. Something was not quite right with Wiley, public relations course or not. It was as if his voice was telling me one thing, but the rest of him wasn't quite agreeing.

"Oh, it's not really that important. I had a quick question for him."

"Fire away; maybe I can help you."

"I had a little thought on a possible other motive for murder. Something that's not as obvious as all these women Manly was playing around with."

"Well, Mrs. Upchurch, don't keep me in suspense. If you've solved the murder, I want to hear all about it."

The patronizing tone of his voice irritated me. He wasn't working real hard to suppress a smile that flitted around the corners of his mouth. For the second time that day, I found myself facing a cocky young man who had never moved out of that stage of development that Erikson characterizes as believing the world revolves around you. It seemed to directly correlate with the size of their muscles. If Bubba and Wiley were any indication of the maturity of their friend, Manly must have been a lot of fun.

"Wiley, I'm wondering if J.C. realizes there is juice flowing over at the Iron Body Health Club."

Wiley's chin dropped and his lips formed an almost perfect *O*. He sat straight up in his chair and almost knocked the Jackson Funeral Home calendar off the wall, dumping all the U.S. presidents' pictures that occupied the top half of the calendar on the floor in the process.

"Mrs. Upchurch, have you been telling this around? You could really get in trouble saying things like that if they're not true."

"Well, for heaven's sake, Wiley, don't get all huffy on me. I didn't say I was going to print it in the paper or anything. Besides, I believe it is the truth. You didn't answer my question. Does J.C. know?"

"Of course Chief Spivey knows about it. You go on home and have a nice Thanksgiving with your family. Like J.C. says, leave law enforcement to the professionals. Those nefarious type criminals can be a real problem for a layman or lady like yourself. Besides, a good lawyer ought to be able to get Mrs. Larue off on involuntary manslaughter."

Wiley sure knew how to make you feel at peace. Wiley and I, we were at the heart of a problem. I was a woman, therefore I needed to go home and be quiet. Cook dinner. Mend some socks. Chivalry is a double-edged sword. There is a breed of man that fusses and fawns, insists on opening doors for you and thinks less of you as a woman if you don't let him. Never mind that you've got three small children at home and there is nobody there to open the doors when you get home from the Food Lion, so you learn to open the door with a toddler on your hip and a bag of groceries in your arms while keeping the three-year-old who is wearing his good shoes out of the wading pool. These are the same men who talk pedestal. To paraphrase something I read a long time back, the person on the pedestal is always allowed to come down long enough to clean the toilets. Nothing makes me madder than to get the old pedestal runaround.

The office was empty except for the two of us. "Wiley, I need to make a phone call. It's private. Okay if I use J.C.'s office?" I tried to sound as casual as possible.

"Help yourself, Mrs. Upchurch." Again he was all smiles.

I went in the office and picked up the phone to call the day-care center and tell them I was running late. While I was waiting, I leafed through a pile of folders on the desk. In deference to my conscience, I looked at only those things that pertained to Angel's case. Nothing of much importance. There were some pictures of Manly's office before the body was removed. I searched through them, looking for something significant. Muscle trophies, video tapes marked on the outside with the letters VHT in red, and varied office paraphernalia filled the photographs. As I finished my call, I heard Wiley's knee knock against the desk as he got up. I pushed the pictures back in the folder and made it to the door before he did. Exclaiming loudly about the time, I breezed by, wishing him a good holiday as I left.

I rushed into Busy Buddies right at six to pick up the children. Jason was impatient. Children are such creatures of habit. I try to get them from day care by five at the latest; sometimes I send Misty Jane by after she gets off work at the hospital at four-thirty. Today had been so crazy I hadn't had time to call anyone to get them for me. You would have thought Jason was a little old lady left at bridge club past pick-up time by the chauffeur. Melissa hung back. A sure sign of trouble.

We picked Becky up at Naomi Petty's house. Naomi and Becky were working on a science fair project together. In the car, I questioned everyone about their day.

"Great."

"Good."

"Okay."

Ask any child a question involving school and he or she can find a way to give you a one-word answer.

"What did you do today?"

"Nothing."

"Did you behave?"

"Uh-huh."

"What did you study?"

"Stuff."

Some days it's hard to imagine that these children are related to me. Upon repeated questioning, Melissa finally produced a note from her teacher, Miss Hudson. The note requested a conference with me concerning Melissa's behavior. The perfect ending to the perfect day.

"Melissa, would you like to tell me what's going on?"

"Nothing."

"Melissa, honey, teachers do not request conferences in the middle of the grading period because they want to share their joy with you. So what is this note for?"

She shook her head and shrugged her shoulders.

"Well, if it comes back to you, let me know. I'm going to find out about it sooner or later. I'd much rather find out from you than from Miss Hudson."

We stopped at the Food Lion on the way home. The phone rang before I could even get my key in the door. The same three children who could not possibly have enough energy to help bring the groceries in all dove for it, screaming, "I've got it!" We lost several eggs in one of the bags in the process. No other damage was sustained, except to Becky's eighth-grade ego. She could not believe it wasn't for her.

It was Vicki reporting on her day. She had visited with Angel.

"Barbara, do you have any idea the kind of people that are in the waiting room at the prison? Oh my, I thought I might hyperventilate at first."

"Nobody there from the church choir, huh?"

"I get shivers thinking about it, Barbara. Angel looked good, if you can imagine being in a place like that and looking good. I think she is being treated extremely well." Vicki cleared her throat. "Speaks well of what people think of our family." I thought it spoke well of how good Angel looked in blue jeans. "One thing that concerns me a bit. Agent Bailey came in while I was there to clear up some points in Angel's statement. I mean, I wasn't going to say anything, but shouldn't Sam Quakenbush be with her if she is going to talk with someone like that?"

"I'm sure that Sam advised her about that, but I'll call him later and double check. I can't understand why Agent Bailey is hanging around. Surely the SBI has processed all the lab work by now." The SBI agents were always pretty efficient, wrapping up their work in short order and going back to Raleigh.

"I hate to bring it up, but Angel was awfully concerned about whether you'd seen Madame Zsa Zsa yet. I tried to sidetrack her by asking her advice on Misty Jane and Dr. Merriwether. She had several good suggestions—"

"That's great Vicki, but we've got a problem." While we talked, I unloaded groceries, putting aside the ingredients I needed for my pecan tarts and broccoli-walnut casserole. Those are the dishes I take every Thanksgiving to Mama and Daddy's. We eat lunch at Mama's and supper with Mrs. Upchurch so Edgar can be there after he finishes hunting.

"Vicki, I can't find a soul who knows the names of Manly Richards's partners in that spa. I'm going to need you to go to Raleigh to the secretary of state's office and go through the incorporations on Friday and find out those names. I'm going to go over and talk with Madame Zsa Zsa and explain to her how our spirits are feeling about her messing with Angel's spirits."

"Barbara Gail, I've been talking with Joe Dan, and he thinks, well, he thinks you ought to let J.C. and Sam Quakenbush handle this situation now." Vicki sounded hesitant. "I mean with Angel and everything. What does Edgar say?"

"Edgar says, 'Do you know if I have any clean blue socks?' and, oh yeah, I guess he did say something about not bailing me out of jail."

"Oh."

"Vicki, are you going to turn your back on your own sister because Joe Dan Macauley is afraid he might miss dinner?"

"No. No, of course not." She didn't sound convinced.

"Besides, tell Joe Dan you're going Christmas shopping. He won't have to know you're going to stop at the secretary of state's office."

I was sure Joe Dan Macauley did not tell her every time he stopped for a plate of barbecue, and that was dangerous for him. In the background, I heard loud sniffing. "Is someone crying?"

"Poor Misty Jane came home all upset. Sharon McLamb called her at work today to invite her to the Hope Class Christmas party. Right after that, she found out that Dr. Merriwether had asked Marilyn Hargrove out for a movie. It was all too much for one day."

I couldn't tell who was more unhappy, Misty Jane or Vicki. "That's a shame, but it's no surprise. Doris Hargrove has been working like a woman possessed to get a hook in Dr. Merriwether. She corners him at every social event. Why, the Sunday he visited at the church, you couldn't even get down the aisle for her blocking it while she was drooling all over him. No one could speak to him without her interrupting to name off some accomplishment of Marilyn's. I guess Doris thinks if she can get a hook in him then she'll hand the pole over to Marilyn to reel him in."

"She is so obvious." Vicki sighed loudly into the phone. It wasn't so much that Doris Hargrove was obvious, it was that whatever she was doing was working.

After we hung up, I got the children settled with some leftover barbecued chicken, salad, and corn while I got the broccoli casserole in the oven. Edgar was out on deer hunting business. He'd have to fend for himself when he got home.

I started on my pecan tarts, but with every ingredient, I became more and more incensed that J.C. Spivey would blatantly disregard this drug thing. I hadn't mentioned it to Vicki on the phone because I wasn't sure where it was leading and I didn't want to talk out of school and get Bubba Pittman in trouble. *If* it could be avoided. No use slinging dirt all over Ladawn's family if it wasn't going to accomplish anything.

For all his good qualities, which I sometimes have trouble naming, J.C. can be pigheaded. This was especially likely to be the case if he thought somebody was telling him how to do his job. I've told him he needs to learn to rely on his intuitive side, not facts alone. He has told me to mind my own business. If he and Agent Bailey had a difference of opinion on anything, maybe I could get one or the other of them to doubt Angel's guilt. I needed to convince somebody to start looking for a new suspect.

I pounded the crusts into the tart cups and silently argued with J.C., occasionally speaking a word out loud for emphasis. Point by point, I showed him how he needed to reconsider. He had his head in the sand on this steroid thing. I was so convincing in my argument that I was sure he would agree.

I dialed the number to his house. Eunice answered the phone. She and J.C. never had any children. Some women replace children with careers or doing good works; Eunice replaced them with crafts and animals. Besides her passion for ceramics and needlework, she also has a menagerie of animals: dogs, cats, and an assortment of rabbits. I explained to her that I was looking for J.C.

"My goodness, Barbara, I don't expect him home for a while."

"Listen, Eunice, could I leave him a message?"

"I'll try to remember it, but I can't promise. We just got a new poodle and I'm trying to make her a Christmas outfit. She's gonna be in the parade next Saturday. I can't seem to get the fit right. Maybe you could call back and speak with J.C. If I drop my hands, Gigi might get away and stick herself with all these pins."

The Lord can think of more ways to test my patience. "No problem, Eunice. I'll talk to him later."

"I don't know what else to tell you. Wiley Bass came by a while ago and I told him to try J.C. on his truck radio, but he said he already had. He seemed to be torn right out of his frame. Got poor Gigi all worked up and she nipped him. You know, poodles are very sensitive animals. I still haven't got her calmed down." I wondered to myself, as I was hanging up the phone, why Wiley would go to see J.C. at home. Friday, right after my trip to see Madame Zsa Zsa, I was going to the station to find out. Maybe there was a new lead in Manly's death.

I looked in the oven and grabbed a potholder. My casserole was on the edge of being too brown; I pulled it from the oven in time to avoid making a new one. The tarts were ready to bake.

If I had that night to go back over, I would have let my broccoli burn, gone without the tarts for Thanksgiving, and worked harder at figuring out why Wiley was looking for J.C. at seven o'clock on Thanksgiving eve. It would have saved Wiley's mama a lot of heartache.

7

Thanksgiving passed in muted celebration. Mama followed her usual habit of cooking twice what she needed for the meal. The children helped with table setting and bringing extra chairs before they went off to the front bedroom, where a TV and video games awaited them. The indulgence of grandparents.

Angel gets her perennial ability to look young from my parents. While they are both in their seventies you would easily guess they were twenty years younger. Daddy still tends a large garden, and Mama cans vegetables and makes various jellies nonstop during harvest. Daddy has become a Nintendo fiend late in life, and all those aggressive feelings he must have put back over the years come out against the enemies of the Mario Brothers. There is a quilt frame in one corner of the living room that always has a project of Mama's stretched out over it. I inherited none of my mama's talent with a needle and thread. We keep a large basket of projects in the laundry room to take to Mama's house for sewing surgery. Recently, Melissa came into the bedroom, where I was replacing a button on her brother's shirt, and remarked, "Mom, I had no idea you could sew."

Angel remained in jail pending a second bail hearing that Sam Quakenbush thought would result in her release on bond. After lunch, Misty Jane stayed at the house with the children while Mama, Daddy, Vicki, and I went off to visit Angel. Edgar was still out on the hunt and Martin, Vicki and Joe Dan's son, went off to take his girlfriend to the movies. He was maturing rapidly, a growth spurt taking him from a relatively skinny kid to a muscular young man.

Vicki sank back against the car seat. "I think that Martin and this Tiffany are altogether too serious for high school seniors. No need to marry first thing out of high school." I wondered if she was thinking about herself and Joe Dan. "Then, of course, look at Misty Jane. I suppose it's feast or famine."

We turned onto Prison Camp Road and Daddy leaned around in his seat. "Did you signal at that last turn, Barbara?"

Mama poked him. "Charles, she's thirty-five years old. If she hasn't learned to drive by now, lessons are not going to help."

We all laughed that sort of tense, high-strung laugh that feels like it's so tight it might pop like a rubber band and come back and hit you. Then we were pulling into the parking lot at the Harnett County Correctional Institute. From the cars we maneuvered through it appeared that every one of the eighty prisoners had at least one visitor. I dropped Mama, Daddy, and Vicki at the sidewalk and found a place to park on down the side road. The waiting area was full and overflowing onto the sidewalk outside. Vicki was right about the crowd. Eclectic would be a nice way to describe it. I pulled the jacket I'd worn tighter around me. The weather was almost springlike, but I couldn't get warm.

I walked in and told the jailer there were four of us to see Angel. The jailer was a woman in her forties who stood behind a rectangular window with a slot at the bottom big enough to pass papers through. Sort of like a movie ticket booth. Four for Angel. The jailer told me it would be a few minutes. After a wait of about thirty minutes, Angel's name was called.

I promised to stay only a few minutes and went in first. The visitor's side of the glass is a long narrow room with phone booth-like partitions separating spaces of glass. Each booth is marked with a metallic number like you would use on your mailbox. Angel was seated in booth four.

My breathing quickened when I saw her sitting there, and I thought how hard it would be for Mama and Daddy to endure this. I sat down on the stainless-steel stool, the smoke from some of the other visitors making me cough. Angel's hair was down around her shoulders. It looked better than mine even though I knew she'd styled it using the stainless-steel mirror on her cell wall. (The stainless-steel mirror having the effect of not being able to tell me from, say, Julia Roberts.) The orange jumpsuit she was wearing courtesy of the county hung loosely on her slender frame. A hint of dark circles under her eyes was the only sign that prison was a problem for her. I pulled my plastic phone off the wall mount. Angel did the same.

"Happy Thanksgiving!" Only Angel was carefree enough to wish me a happy Thanksgiving while she was a guest of the county.

"Same to you, hon. Are you doing all right? Do you have enough money?" Edgar had left money for her when he came to the bond hearing on Tuesday. Prisoners' money is kept in a fund that they can draw from for snacks and drinks three times a day. Angel nodded yes to both questions.

"It's kind of lonely being in that cell all the time. It's a good thing I'm such a spiritually centered person. You know, solitude has always been important to spirituality." *This* was my sister? She twirled her hair. "Course, I wouldn't mind going dancing at the Longbranch." *This* was my sister. "Have you been able to see Madame Zsa Zsa yet?"

"No, Angel, I haven't. I don't want to discourage you, but the woman wouldn't even see me until tomorrow morning. I'm telling you, Angel, the woman's a flake. To put it gently, she does not have your best interests at heart."

"Barb, you know it's important to me. Manly always said she was a true visionary."

I slapped the steel counter in front of me. The guy in booth five jumped several inches. "You mean Madame Zsa Zsa knew Manly?"

"Really Barb, I told you Manly was a man of the nineties. Yes, he knew her. You are still going to see her, aren't you?" It never occurred to Angel that the madame might be suspect.

"Of course I'll go see her, but you've got to promise me one thing."

"Sure, why not?"

"Mama, Daddy, and Vicki are here with me and you've got to promise you won't say a word to them about any of this. They're all worried sick and I can't go off chasing Madame Zsa Zsa if I've got to tend to one of them in the hospital. You promise."

She looked hurt. "Of course I promise. What do you think I'd do anyway?"

I wouldn't want to guess.

"By the way, I can have paperbacks to read. Could you bring me some? No trashy stuff, either; maybe some classics like, well, you'll know some good ones."

This was a new twist; Angel was not a reader. "I'll make sure we get you some. Are you really okay, honey?"

"As fine as I'll be in here. All this time to think makes me realize I've relied on my looks too much. I need to develop my brain. I could be as smart as you if I tried."

"I know you could. You've just never seemed to be very interested." For some reason, this made her mad.

"Like I had a choice. You were the smart one; I had to be cute. It was all there was left."

I didn't want to ask what options this gave Vicki. "I'm going on out and let the others come in."

"Don't worry, I'm not going anywhere."

Angel must have kept her promise. Mama and Daddy were teary eyed, but everyone agreed Angel was holding up well under the circumstances.

By the time we finished at the prison, it was close to four o'clock. I planned to drop Vicki, Mama, and Daddy off at the house, gather up my children, and go on over to the Upchurches' house to wait for the mighty hunters to return so we could eat again. Not that I needed to eat anything; by this time my Easy Rider jeans were not riding so easy.

I'd started to back out of the driveway when Becky remarked, "I think Granddaddy wants you."

Daddy was standing on the porch signaling something with his hands. "One of y'all must have left something. Becky, run see what it is."

Instead of going back in the house to retrieve the forgotten item, Daddy came around to my side of the car. "Martin's been in an accident. They think he's all right, but they have him over at Northern Harnett."

Before he finished his sentence I could feel a rush of adrenaline hit my system. I said a prayer for Martin as we all tumbled back out of the car and into the house.

Vicki was standing in the living room with her face stark white and a sort of falsetto tone to her voice. "I can't find my pocketbook. Has anyone seen my pocketbook? It was here a second ago."

Jason spied it on the floor by the chair Vicki was sitting in when we'd left the house what seemed like an hour ago.

The whole way to the hospital, Vicki worked her hands round and round, reminding me of the motion that Granny B. makes when she goes out of her head and thinks that she's back working bobbins in the mill. "I wonder if he'll need to be moved to Raleigh. He's so careful with that car of his, treats it like a baby. I can't believe he wrecked it."

"Vicki, you know there are a lot of crazies on the road." I pulled another tissue from my purse and handed it to her, barely missing a mailbox in the process. Vicki never noticed.

"The shock will probably put Joe Dan in the bed right beside him."

"Maybe not. Joe Dan's heart is stronger than we think." A lot stronger than he thinks, but no need to get into that now.

Misty Jane's car pulled into the parking lot behind us. Mama and Daddy were home with the children. No need for everyone to converge at the hospital. I promised I'd call when we knew anything, and Mama said she would call Mrs. Upchurch and let her know what was going on.

The emergency room at Northern Harnett was quiet. No one had overdosed on Thanksgiving yet. Misty Jane called the clerk behind the window by name. The woman was about Misty Jane's age; her nametag identified her as Elaine. Elaine was obviously bored at having to work the holiday and had been catching up on her reading. The latest Danielle Steel novel was lying open on the desk beside her.

Elaine acknowledged Misty Jane. "The accident victim is your brother? I had no idea."

At the designation of Martin as an accident victim, fresh tears started down Vicki's face.

"Now, Mama, it's okay." Misty Jane gave Elaine a cautioning look. Elaine proved to be an adept observer of human nature.

"Oh sure, he's gonna be just fine. I've seen them in a lot worse shape than him. Why the other night we had a guy in—"

"Misty Jane, why don't you stay and get forms filled out and your mom and I will walk on back and see Martin." I interrupted Elaine.

"Oh sure, he's second door to the right. I'll page the

doctor." Elaine appeared only slightly miffed at not getting to finish her story.

"Now, Vicki," I lectured as we went down the hall, "you've got to be strong for Martin's sake. Going in there and crying is only going to make matters worse."

Martin was lying on a gurney with a sheet pulled to his shoulders. Beside him, a nurse fiddled with the IV drip that was going into his arm. He was wearing one of those blue hospital gowns and had a bandage going around the top of his head that covered most of his dark hair. His face was an assortment of cuts at odd angles across his nose, cheeks, and chin. With his severe case of acne, it looked like someone had tried to play connect the dots.

The nurse looked up and acknowledged us with a curt smile. "He's a little distressed so we gave him a sedative. He should be able to rest better now."

When he saw his mother he started to cry. I braced myself to handle the two of them.

"Martin, honey, it's gonna be fine. Bless your heart, you have banged yourself up but good." Vicki had pulled herself together and was leaning over the gurney, kissing Martin's cheek and using her hand to keep him from trying to sit up.

I couldn't help but be impressed with the effects of my lecture.

"Mama, Tiffany broke up with me. She doesn't want to see me again. I can't stand it, Mama. I love her. I can't stand . . ." His voice trailed off in a series of sobs.

Vicki leaned close and soothed him with quiet words until his sobbing subsided into little catches of breath. She plumped his pillows and turned to me, a mama bear protecting her cub. "I've never liked that

Tiffany," she whispered in a self-righteous tone. "She's trouble, I told Joe Dan—"

I reached out and squeezed her arm and gave her a warning look. Behind her, Martin, in control of his tears, turned his head to listen.

"I'm sure this is going to work out." I moved around her and gave Martin a light kiss. His hand came up to find mine and the grip relaxed as the sedative began its work.

A noise came from the doorway and we turned to find a young woman with short red hair and a pixie look standing with a chart in her hand. She moved towards us. "Mrs. Macauley?"

Vicki stepped towards her. "I'm Mrs. Macauley," she said reaching a hand up to smooth her hair.

The young woman nodded. "I'm Dr. Patterson." She smiled pleasantly and looked at me. I have to admit I was not prepared for her to be the doctor. Old concepts die hard. I had been so embarrassed when Mr. Upchurch kept asking before his heart surgery, "Who is that little foreign girl keeps running around here?" That little foreign girl was head of the surgery team. And here I was automatically thinking this young woman was another nurse instead of the doctor.

"I'm Barbara Upchurch, Mrs. Macauley's sister."

Misty Jane appeared in the doorway. She was biting her bottom lip and twisting her hands. I had a vision of Vicki at her age. "Aunt Barbara, could you come out here for a minute?"

As soon as I got into the hall and saw the highway patrolman standing there, my heart started to beat a little faster. I hadn't smelled any alcohol when I leaned down to kiss Martin. Surely he wasn't drinking and driving.

Misty Jane motioned me down and introduced me to Officer Lee Ellis.

"Ma'am, I was asking Miss Macauley here if her brother seemed to be distraught. Everything he's told me about the accident, well, it doesn't add up." He looked at Misty Jane and then back toward me. "Quite frankly, I think he ran into that tree on purpose."

I felt like I got on the merry-go-round for a quick spin and somebody had locked it into high gear. Everything was spinning, and those horses were going up and down. Before I could say anything, Vicki and Dr. Patterson walked into the hall. From behind us came the noise of Joe Dan arriving in the reception area. He had brought along his mother, a short, gray woman with emotional diarrhea. She proceeded to grab Vicki by the neck and cry, "How is he? How is he?" between sobs, obviously not expecting anyone to tell her, since she never paused for a breath. Misty Jane pulled her off Vicki, who took a moment to catch her breath and straighten her dress, a sailor style that I'd never seen made up in a print fabric before. The square collar was edged in rickrack.

Misty Jane continued to back Mrs. Macauley out of the circle. "Now Granny, he's going to be all right, but you aren't going to be able to see him if you keep on like this." I was impressed. Misty Jane was becoming a regular pillar.

Dr. Patterson and the highway patrolman stepped away for a quick conference. The doctor turned to us.

"Mr. and Mrs. Macauley, I'd like to speak with you alone if I could."

Divide and conquer, now that was a plan. I stepped toward the patrolman in hope of getting some more information. Elaine came down the hall holding her finger in her paperback to mark her place.

"Lee, you're wanted on the phone." She smiled coyly at the patrolman. Nothing like a man in uniform.

A strangled sob came from my right. Dr. Patterson supported Vicki by her elbow and they moved towards the green vinyl chairs that lined the wall. Joe Dan had a hand clutched over his heart like he was getting ready to pledge the flag.

Mrs. Macauley pulled away from Misty Jane. "What? What?"

I shook my head at Misty Jane. The last thing Vicki needed was Mrs. Macauley falling over her again. Misty Jane stepped out of her mild-mannered daughter persona. "Granny, why don't you and me go on down here to the Coke machine and get us a drink?" She had her hand on Mrs. Macauley's back, nudging her past the chairs where Vicki, Joe Dan, and Dr. Patterson now sat.

Vicki motioned for me. Dr. Patterson was patting Vicki's hand. "We won't know for sure until we get the blood test back, but the physical signs are fairly conclusive."

Vicki looked up teary-eyed. "The doctor thinks Martin has been taking steroids."

"Steroids?" This whole thing was getting crazier by the minute. How was Martin getting steroids, and why?

Dr. Patterson nodded. "The development of certain physical characteristics: thick shaggy hair on his arms and legs, a heavy case of acne, and the development of breasts that somewhat resemble female breasts."

At this Joe Dan let out a loud humph.

Dr. Patterson ignored him. "Synthetic hormones may cause the body to quit producing its own testosterone, the male hormone, thus causing the development of female characteristics. Often steroid users are given to sudden rages, like the one Martin experienced that caused him to ram his car into a tree. Fortunately for him, the patrolman said his seatbelt and his car's low speed saved him."

What a mess. No wonder Martin had gone from a skinny kid to a Mr. Clean lookalike. Poor Vicki and Joe Dan; they resembled two lost puppies.

"The good news," Dr. Patterson continued, "is that steroids are not addictive in the traditional sense of the word. People get addicted to the need to develop more and more muscle, but not to the drug itself."

"That's encouraging." I smiled at Vicki. This was getting more and more complicated all the time. J.C. Spivey had better figure out what was going on, and fast. News of Martin's problem would not sit well with parents of high school students. I wasn't sure what to do. What if Bubba had more information? And I had to find out the names of the Iron Body partners. Maybe they knew something about all this. Every time I thought this stuff was about to get easier, it just got more complicated. I kept getting more questions instead of more answers. This was not the way it was supposed to work.

Vicki grabbed my hand. "What are we going to do?"

This was definitely not the way it was supposed to work. Thanksgiving was a day to eat as much as you could before your stomach completely gave up the ghost. Not, I repeat, not to go visit one sister in prison and take the other to the hospital to visit her son who tried to kill himself over some stringy-haired girl from Mamers, the cause of his condition most likely being that the incarcerated sister's dead boyfriend had sold him drugs. I wondered if I could talk Dr. Patterson into a Valium for the road. I wished I knew what to do for everyone, but, honestly, I wanted to be in charge of the Christmas parade, not everyone's life.

I couldn't wait to get to Madame Zsa Zsa. If she couldn't help me with Angel, the least she could do was tell me how many people I had killed in my last life to deserve this.

Joe Dan let out a loud belch and patted Vicki on the shoulder. "I think I'm gonna take Mama on home and take me a heart pill. I need to lay down and rest."

No doubt.

8

By the time Misty Jane and Vicki worked out a schedule for sitting with Martin, Mama and Daddy had arrived. When he got out of the woods at dusk, Edgar had picked up the children and taken them on to his mom's. I made Vicki and Misty Jane promise to call if there was any change, but the doctor felt Martin was in decent shape and his stay was for observation.

When I got to the Upchurches', supper was over. Mrs. Upchurch insisted on fixing me a plate that overflowed its sides and on wrapping coconut cake for me to take home when I protested that I had no room left for anything else. Then she packed us a basket for the road.

The children settled in for the night with little sibling quibbling. Edgar went off to the kitchen to make some decaf and I peeled off the jeans and sweater I'd worn, wishing that I could peel away the cares of the day with them. I reached into the closet and pulled my

oversize cotton T-shirt and harem pants off the hook
inside the door. The cotton against my skin and the
cool wood floor on my bare feet were like a tonic.

This was the kind of day that made me sorry Edgar
and I had decided to turn down the permanent corporate position in Connecticut. We had lived there for
about six months one time after Becky was born, but
felt like we wanted to get closer to home to raise children. Edgar had been the talk of the office when he
turned down the position. Edgar, a man ahead of his
time. (Who knew then that work versus family would
become the issue of the nineties? Certainly not Edgar;
he knew where he wanted to hunt.)

One trip to Macy's the day after Thanksgiving cured
my Yankee fever. When the woman next to me at the
sale table took a sweater right out of my hands, I started
whistling "Dixie." Then you have those people who talk
real slow to you, like you can't understand English.
They want to know things like do we have Christmas
trees in the South. "Well, I'm sure we would," I'd tell
them, "*if* we only celebrated Christmas."

I thought as I checked on all the children that if we
were in Connecticut right now I would just be making
sympathetic noises into the phone. As I adjusted
Joshua's cover, the other voice in my head, the realist,
said, *Oh no you wouldn't; you'd be on an airplane flying down here while Edgar fed the kids Raisin Bran
three meals a day*.

The kitchen was quiet except for the hiss and burble
of the coffeemaker. Edgar was wearing a red-and-
white sweatsuit with NCSU emblazoned down the leg.
He is a bit over six feet, with broad shoulders and a
nice behind. His salt-and-pepper hair has more gray at

the temples than brunette. It gives him a certain dignity, even when he is wearing tree-bark camouflage or a sweatsuit. He jogs semi-regularly (every other month) and plays men's softball on the mill team. They let him have his way because he is the boss. Despite his efforts to stay in shape, his body has lost the hard lines of youth and rounds softly, almost unnoticeably, at his waist. It isn't such a bad thing; the razor-thin corners of his personality are also softening. I don't cut myself nearly so often on them, and he would probably say the same of me.

He turned as he pulled mugs from the cabinet to smile at me. "Long day, huh?"

"I'm seriously considering taking up hunting. Where else can you go and hide for an entire day?"

He sat a steaming cup of coffee in front of me. "No fair; I sat through the bail hearing. That should count for something."

"You must look like a shady character, since Angel was denied bail."

"Purely a travesty of justice. But speaking of hunting, I do think the country air is good for you. It'll put the full bloom of youth back in those cheeks."

"So they look old." I smacked the air around his face with my hand. He caught my wrist and lightly kissed my hand.

"Now don't put words in my mouth."

"And don't think you're fooling me; I know what that country air stuff is all about."

The last few months we had argued—excuse me, discussed—whether to use some savings as a down payment on a piece of land in the country. Edgar was in some sort of midlife crisis. It had begun in the last few months of his thirty-ninth year and ballooned into a full-fledged state of emergency at forty. The cure seemed to hinge on us moving to the country, raising animals, and growing our own food. This was not okay with me. If I'd wanted to be a farmer's wife I would have married somebody who was going to inherit the back forty, not someone with a degree in textile engineering. Go for the Scarlett O'Hara look, as opposed to Sally Field in *Places in the Heart*. Edgar had gotten the children on his side with promises of horses. This only made me more opposed. I knew who would be feeding "My Friend Flicka" when the fun wore off, not to mention providing taxi service for every ballgame, sleepover, and homecoming float meeting. The other one of us would have to work late at the mill, at the *important* job.

Edgar grinned. "Well, at least it's not a Porsche like Mike Bickham bought or a twenty-year-old like Steve Chapman divorced Marianne for last year."

"Nor is it a diamond anniversary band like Ellen Floyd, Julie Sullivan, Katherine Carter, or Melody Brock got last year," I said ticking off the names on my fingers. This was my answer to the request for country living. I wanted a diamond anniversary ring. It sounds petty and it is, but I had waited patiently for the last three years for Edgar to think of it all by himself. When he missed my little hints, I gave up and outright told him. I wanted a little romance, flowers some other time besides our anniversary, or a surprise weekend away now and then.

He pulled my hand up and guided me over to his lap on the other side of the table. "But I show my affection for you all the time. You don't need some materialistic display to know I love you." He put his arms around me.

"No, but now and then I would like a Christmas present that didn't come from aisle five of the Revco." (A slight exaggeration on my part.)

"Since when did you start wanting to wear some diamond band for show? You don't even like jewelry."

"Wrong. I don't even like cheap jewelry. Cubic zirconia and all that. Besides, people can change."

"Well, it's out of the question this year. We've got to save all our money to help your criminally insane sister."

That was unnecessary. "Then I guess we sure couldn't buy a piece of land or get a new redbone coonhound." Edgar had been making loud statements about purchasing a $10,000 redbone coonhound. His dogs were getting old, he said. "I'm the only woman I know that can say, yes, my husband went through midlife crisis so I've got a dog that cost more that my children and I live in the middle of nowhere." I pushed myself up off his lap.

"Now come on, Barbara, you know I was kidding about your sister. You know yourself she is skating on very thin ice."

He was right, but that didn't mean I was going to admit to it. Then I remembered that, with Vicki out of the picture, I was going to need someone to go to the secretary of state's office on Friday.

I sat back down on his lap and nuzzled his neck. "I do need a favor tomorrow."

He pushed back my shoulders. I was trying not to laugh.

"I knew it. I knew when this thing started the bail

hearing would be the beginning, and God only knows where it will all end."

"It's nothing really. I mean, I know I've asked you to help out a time or two."

"A time or two? A time or two? What do you call the Walk for World Peace and the auction for the children's home? I seem to remember some very late nights and heavy lifting involved, and that was only in the last year. Honestly, Barbara, I love you, but you always take on more than is humanly possible. You cannot overcompensate for the rest of your family and the free world."

I swung my legs back and forth. "Does that mean you'll take the children to the movies in Raleigh tomorrow and look up the Iron Body incorporation at the secretary of state's office while you're there?"

He pretended to bang his forehead with the heel of his hand. "Of course it does."

I leaned over and kissed him. "Thanks so much. You could even go by the mall and look at diamond anniversary rings while you're there."

He kissed me back. "You won't need one out on the farm."

It was late. I let him have the last word.

It seemed only minutes from the time I put my head on the pillow until the radio woke me. The strains of "Stand by Your Man" played in my ear. I was annoyed that the one day the children were out of school I had to get up early, and I fought the temptation to pull the covers off of Edgar. He was going to go by the secretary of state's office, so I resisted and crawled from under the comforter toward the shower.

No matter how much he grumbled, Edgar knew the handwriting was on the wall. There would be no peace or dinner until I made sense out of what was going on. To be honest, he had also seen the effect this whole thing was having on Mama and Dad, and I think he was half hoping I'd stir something up that would help Angel go free. Much as he fussed about my family, he did go out of his way to watch out for Mama and Daddy.

I wondered as I toweled off in the cool bathroom if I was going to get any useful information from Madame Zsa Zsa; maybe she would give me the psychic lowdown on Manly and the club. At the very least, I hoped my trip to see Madame Zsa Zsa would get all this karma stuff off Angel's mind and help her concentrate on what she knew that would assist the rest of us in getting her out of jail.

I ran my fingers through my brown hair to fluff the perm Lucille had given me. I couldn't wait until my hair grew enough to cut the perm out. Perms were always a good idea until they were in your hair. My eyebrows were getting shaggy, so I reached into the shower to get my pink razor and shaved the stray hairs at the top of my nose and above my eyes. I'd given up plucking my eyebrows after I had my first child; waste of time. I pulled on a denim jumper and a turquoise cotton turtleneck and snuck into Becky's room and borrowed her Esprit half boots. The effect was middle-aged bohemian, the best I could do for Madame Zsa Zsa.

I poured a cup of coffee into my green plastic Dash Mart cup and headed off to a rural area outside of Erwin off Highway 55.

The house sat off a dirt road in the middle of some tobacco fields. It was a wood frame whose only concession to its cosmic owner was its pink color. The smell of ginger and sandalwood met me before I had time to shut my car door. It wrapped around the entire wooden railed porch like a screen. On the side of the porch was parked a new Lincoln. *Business must be good*, I thought.

Strong perfumes make my eyes water and my nose stop up. Musty houses give me sinus problems. I knew as soon as I set foot in Madame Zsa Zsa's I would have to take a decongestant before the day was over. The living room was filled with overstuffed chairs and a couch, in mismatched floral prints. The dust rose up in a cloud when Madame Zsa Zsa swept the cat off to make room for me to sit down.

Both she and the cat, a white Persian, appeared not to have missed any meals. I was surprised at the agility of both, considering their size. Madame Zsa Zsa moved with cat-like grace and one sensed that, lurking behind her green eyes, she had the ability to pounce on her prey at a moment's notice.

She was wrapped in what appeared to be a blue mumu with a woven multicolored belt around the middle. The color of her vibrant red hair was not a naturally occurring phenomenon. It flowed to her shoulders, half covering earrings big enough to serve lunch on. The first four inches on each arm were adorned with bracelets that tinkled together when she moved her hands to talk.

"Madame Zsa Zsa, I'll come right to the point. Our family is very concerned for Angel."

She shook her head and muttered to herself, "Tragic, tragic!"

"We feel that since her association began with you, she has not been herself. While we appreciate you renewing Angel's sense of the spiritual, we are unhappy with some things that are happening."

The last time Angel had gotten the spirit, she was eleven. We had gone to a kind of outdoor tent revival known as a camp meeting with Uncle Robert and his family. A camp meeting is a place where people fall under the spirit, shout out, and speak in tongues. Being raised mainline Baptist, where such displays have been replaced by an occasional amen, we were shocked when Angel jumped up, raised her hands, and shouted. We all thought she had the spirit for sure. Turns out she was wearing sandals and Cousin Bert had stepped on her toe with his cowboy boot.

"You must understand that Angel is ridding herself of this very unnatural red in her karma. It takes much time."

"It also seems to take much money."

She eyed me, pursing her lips. "Did not Jesus say, 'But what will a man profit if he gains the world, but loses his soul?'"

Now she was trying to mix religions on me. I folded my hands and met her look. "I don't know my Bible as well as I used to, but I think he might also have said, 'A fool and his money are soon parted.'"

She thought this over. "I have nothing but concern for Angel. What would you have me do?"

"Send her a note, anything to settle her down. She's a grown woman and I can't stop her from giving you money, but I can check your background to see if the county might have concerns over your business." I made a mental note to talk J.C. into getting a computer check on the madame. She looked at me, but made no comment. "And I understand you knew Manly Richards, too. I'd appreciate any information you could give me on him. If you really care about Angel, you'll do something constructive to help her until we can get her out of jail."

"I will try. But from the first time Manly brought her to me, this unnatural red was strong."

"Manly introduced Angel to you?" I'd assumed that it was the other way around.

"But of course. He longed for her to have spiritual wholeness. I was able to talk with her dear departed husband, Lawrence, and put some issues to rest between them."

Lawrence (Larry) was the name of Angel's last husband, Lawrence Lee Larue, who several years ago drove down that great celestial four lane to his heavenly reward when he passed a group of stopped cars in his Lance delivery truck and never realized they were waiting for a drawbridge that had just started to go up. Folks in the cars that he passed said the bridge was at about a thirty-degree incline when he went over the edge and plunged into the Cape Fear River. Packages of Lance nabs were floating everywhere. (Nabs are what we call those cheese and peanut butter snack crackers here in Harnett County.) The orange ones were especially easy to spot, according to what Ed Massey told the *Daily Record*. They got an exclusive on the story and called it, "Cape Fear Nabs Truck Driver." To this day, I can't ever see an orange nab without thinking of Larry. Especially since Angel had City Florist make up a casket spray using various assorted packages of Lance nabs and cookies. I mean, it was a piece of work. Folks talked about it for months.

I nodded at Madame Zsa Zsa. "I'm sure you did talk to Lawrence. And it truly is touching what a thoughtful guy that Manly was. Did you read for him, too?"

"Most certainly."

"Did you give him a group discount for his girlfriends?"

"No, but I did provide him with a small finder's fee for new clients."

The man was a complete bottom-of-the barrel lowlife. "By chance, did he mention his partners to you?"

"No. We did talk of the partnership occasionally, but no names. There were some problems."

"Such as?"

"Money. It truly is the root of all evil."

It was touching. The madame and Manly were trying to rid the world of all the evil they could by getting as much of everyone's money as possible.

"Did Manly ever mention using steroids to you?" Maybe she was his supplier; I couldn't picture her as a partner in the health club.

"No, never. But I suspected there was something wrong. His karma was full of blackness."

"No disrespect intended, but if Manly was in mortal danger, why didn't you see it?"

"I sensed danger, but, alas, I could not see the complete picture. I've been trying to speak to Manly since his death, but those channels seem to be blocked."

"We've been having a lot of trouble with our reception, too."

Before I could get out my next question, Madame Zsa Zsa's eyes rolled back and she swooned backwards, floating towards the floor on the air inside the caftan.

I jumped up, thinking she was going to slide on

down to the floor. I knew if she got down, I'd never get her back up. She was surprisingly light, and I maneuvered her to a half-sitting position on the floor. I fanned her with an issue of the *National Inquirer* that was laying on the table. She rolled her eyes open to look at me.

"I see evil."

"I know. Lucille did a lousy job on this perm, didn't she?"

She squinted up at me. "I had a vision of death."

Manly was dead four days and now she saw death. I suppose having me there had improved her reception. "What sort of vision?"

"It is not clear enough. I must concentrate. I must focus. You must help me." She stuck her finger in my face, setting off a tinkling of bracelets.

My track record at seances and the like isn't very good. The last time I participated in one, I was about ten years old. Vicki, myself, and four of our cousins sat in the dark in Granny B.'s living room. Cousin Margaret, who had been well versed in communicating with the dead by one of her classmates, was enlightening us. Cousin Margaret found the lucky egg every Easter and based on that achievement carried herself with the air of a champion. We were arguing over whether we ought to hold hands or not when the screen door banged and the front door swung open and a large white apparition appeared. There was general squealing and thumping as we tried to fit six abreast out the living room door and down the hall to our parents. The idea of talking with the dead was appealing, but not if they were going to arrive in the same manner as the Avon lady. Returning to the living room accompanied by grinning parents, we found Aunt Easta sitting on the floor, gasping for breath and holding her sides. A sheet was wrapped around her shoulders. I wondered where Madame Zsa Zsa kept her sheets.

"Exactly what is it I have to do?"

That question led to me being seated in a yellow vinyl kitchen chair around what I suspected was Madame Zsa Zsa's all-purpose talk-to-the-dead and dining room table. I kept catching my watchband in the red-lace tablecloth. Candles lit the dining room which she'd darkened by drawing the shades. We were holding hands, but I kept having to rub mine on my dress, since they were sweating. Must have been the room temperature. I knew this was all perfectly ridiculous, but I hadn't quite convinced my sweat glands of that. I shivered involuntarily, and Madame Zsa Zsa opened an eye to look at me. I smiled.

The madame started to talk. Her voice had this singsong quality to it. It was a cross between the man who sold Veg-a-matics at the state fair and a Catholic priest I'd heard recite prayers at Marianne Walters's wedding. Marianne's mother is still not over her getting married and converting to Catholicism all in the same breath.

"I see death. I see a body." She was going to have to do better than that. Anybody who could read a newspaper knew this stuff.

"The body is beside a road, a deserted road. It is a man's body. I cannot see his face. He is on his stomach and the grass covers his face. The light from his jacket, it blinds me."

I opened an eye and peeked at the madame. Angel

could make friends with people who were hanging on to reality by the slimmest thread. Of course, Angel didn't even bother to hold on to the thread.

"I see evil. Evil is a black bag. The black bag radiates evil."

"What's in the black bag?"

"I cannot see. It is not permitted."

Sure, that's convenient. "Okay, then who does it belong to?"

"I do not know. It is not permitted that I know."

"The spirits are going to have to realize we are short on time here. We could use a hint. Pocketbook or briefcase? I need more information."

She still had her eyes closed. "It's fading."

I wondered if I was going to be asked for twenty dollars to reverse the evil black bag's fade into oblivion.

"It's gone. But wait, by another adviser, I am permitted to see Angel. She is smiling. She is dressed for her wedding."

My sweaty palms had dried out. This was no prediction, this was fact. I'm sure even if Angel were to end up on death row that wouldn't stop her from tying the matrimonial knot again. Trouble was, she tied a slip knot every time.

Madame Zsa Zsa pitched forward. I studied her face for a sign of squeezed eyes or nervous ticks. If this was her way of trying to tell me something about the murder without getting herself in trouble, she was doing a good job. I shook her. It took a moment for her eyes to focus on me.

"Can't you get these people or spirits or advisers or whatever they are to be a little more specific? This is important. So important that other indiscretions might be overlooked if someone had essential information."

Madame Zsa Zsa shrugged. "The spirit world only allows us to see what we need to know." She sat up straight and smoothed the wrinkles in her caftan.

Trust Angel to hook up with a madame whose spiritual advisers didn't have an eye for detail—not that I believed Madame Zsa Zsa anyway.

Once again, I secured her promise to send Angel a note letting her know that her karma was salvageable. Then I left to go check with J.C. about new leads. It wouldn't hurt for him to get the state to run a computer check on Madame Zsa Zsa and Bunny Richards.

The road back towards town was empty. To pass the time, I kept trying to picture how an evil black bag would look. Would it be more like Doris Hargrove's black patent Sunday purse or Mitchell's black leather backpack?

I passed over a bridge overhung on both sides with large oak trees that were still in the process of shedding their leaves. Brown and defiant, they swayed in the small breeze that was blowing. I looked around at the passing fields. They were barren with the coming winter. A shanty or barn appeared occasionally in the landscape, but the empty fields bordered by woods seemed to go on forever. Occasionally, there was a field of cotton plants littered with white where the machine that picked the field had left blooms. My granny often told me, "My daddy would have beat my tail end if I'd left that much cotton on a row." It did seem a waste, but the machines must be more cost effective.

The road was more deserted than I remembered. I

glanced nonchalantly at both sides. No bodies could be seen lying in the passing ditches, still lush and green. The weather had not announced the arrival of winter. The trees were the only heralds of what was to come. The squirrels believed them and scampered madly about, picking up acorns.

I sped up the car and locked the doors. That singsongy voice and those candles in the dining room were enough to give you the willies if you let them. Every spooky feeling I'd had in my childhood seemed to come back to me. I passed a possum stretched out on the shoulder of the road. Its glassy eyes looked up at me. If it weren't for a spot of matted red hair on its belly, I might have expected it to roll over and run into the woods. I punched the Mary Chapin Carpenter tape into the player and turned it up. How silly I was being, I told myself. The madame would be proud to know she had gotten to me this much. And Edgar wanted to move out into the country. Sure, just me and old Bessie.

I felt better when I saw the Dash Mart come into view. The station wagon was on empty and I was craving a peanut bar. Peanut bars were my latest candy itch. I justified my purchases by making sure the candy included at least one nutritious ingredient. I had exhausted all the candies with raisins in them, going through one variety about every six months. I was now on to peanuts. I figured I'd have a couple of more years at least before I got through all the peanut candies. Besides, I thought to myself as I pulled up to the gas pumps, I hadn't eaten breakfast before I went to see Madame Zsa Zsa.

Norton Maxwell was behind the counter. He was a

short, bearded man who wore his Dash Mart nametag like a medal. This was Norton's retirement job. He'd retired from the mill several years ago. After two months at home, his wife Eloise told him either he got a job or she was going to; she couldn't take it anymore. In his position as counter clerk, he is a lightning rod for good gossip. "Well, I suppose you heard."

"Heard what?" I put my peanut bar and Diet Mountain Dew up on the counter.

"You know. The news about the body. It's all over town." He rung up my purchase. "Eleven-fifty-nine."

"Which body are you talking about?" I handed him two ten dollar bills.

He chuckled. "Like there is ten or twenty to choose from." He was counting change, enjoying himself thoroughly.

"Come on, Norton. What body are you talking about?"

He took his time, since he knew he had me a virtual captive. He handed me my change and cupped his hand around the side of his mouth and leaned across the counter, I guess to keep the Pine State milk from hearing since there wasn't anyone else in the store.

"Wiley Bass."

"Wiley Bass is dead?" It couldn't be.

"Sure is. You don't think I'd refer to him as a body if he wasn't, do you? They found him out near Raven Rock Park in a ditch alongside the road."

I tried to remember if Madame Zsa Zsa had a police scanner radio. It would explain her vision of the body. "There wasn't a black bag close by, was there?"

"Not that I heard." He shook his head. "Terrible thing, terrible thing."

"Do they know who did it?"

"Buck was pretty tight-lipped when he came by on his way to meet the body truck. J.C. was afraid they'd never find the road without some help. I had to feed Buck three sausage biscuits to get him to tell me they think it's a hit and run."

"Sure, and I'm Princess Di!"

Norton ignored my outburst. "You think Buck is tight-lipped? Be durned if I can get that Agent Bailey to talk at all. He was in here Wednesday night around midnight, fidgeting around, but talking to him is like trying to talk to Eloise after we've had a fight. You may as well spray down your counters and restock your shelves cause you're not going to get him to say a word."

That was crazy. Agent Bailey should have been home Wednesday night at midnight. What was he doing hanging around? It didn't make sense.

Norton kept on talking in spite of the fact that I was not listening. I interrupted in mid-sentence. "What road?"

"Barbara, they were not on a road. They were in the main aisle of Martinsboro First Presbyterian Church."

"Norton, what road did they find Wiley on?"

"State Road 3137. Turn about two miles past Raven Rock Road."

I grabbed my drink and peanut bar, telling Norton I'd hear about the hat incident at First Presbyterian later. It was plain to me, if not to everyone else, that Wiley was not the victim of an accident.

9

The location of Wiley's body was easy to spot. The body truck, the medical examiner's car, two Martinsboro police cars, and the crime lab van marked the spot. Uniforms and suits were everywhere. Agent Bailey stood talking to J.C. I approached them, picking my way over the marshy spots that developed in the ground the closer you got to the ditch beside the road. I was glad I'd worn boots.

"I guess this will give you clues to your other suspects in Manly Richards's murder."

J.C. looked annoyed. "Barbara, I'll recheck the record, but I don't remember Wiley confessing to killing Manly or knowing his killer before he died. I've got plenty of troubles losing a man like this to a hit-and-run without you get your shorts in a knot over something that ain't even your concern." The madder J.C. became the more his grammar suffered.

"J.C., it is my concern. Particularly since you refuse

to comprehend the situation. What we have here is a second murder."

"What we have here is a hit-and-run. Period. End of discussion. Mitchell Hardison has already gotten everything we are giving to the press at the moment." J.C. chopped one hand into his palm, emphasizing every word.

"I suppose this is what they mean by 'blind justice.'"

He glanced sideways at Agent Bailey. "You've been reading too many Nancy Drew books. Some old boy was celebrating Thanksgiving early and beaned Wiley. Best we can tell it was late Wednesday night or early Thursday morning. Rolled him into the ditch and left him. Not premeditated, but plain stupid. That's all."

That was very reassuring, coming from a man whose department thought serial killers eat corn flakes for breakfast. It seemed as good a time as any to get some answers. "Agent Bailey must not think Angel's case is wrapped up. He was down here Wednesday night working while you were out preparing for the big hunt."

Agent Bailey's face flushed. "No, I wasn't."

I opened my mouth to tell him that Norton had seen him, but decided to wait. I couldn't figure out what he was trying to pull.

He excused himself to go talk to the crime lab team. J.C. was red-faced. "Thank you so much, Miss I-Know-It-All. It ain't enough for you to run down my department in front of the man. Oh no, you've got to accuse him of sneaking around the county behind my back."

"For your information, Norton Maxwell says Agent Bailey was in the Dash Mart late Wednesday night. It doesn't take much to figure out something is going on for him to stand here and deny it."

J.C. muttered an unflattering remark about Norton's reliability. I ignored him.

"Barbara, this ain't nothing to do with Angel. You are paying Sam Quakenbush to defend her. Let him. You keep messing around where you don't belong, you're going to get run over, fall in the ditch, or something else you probably deserve. Then everybody's gonna blame me for not stopping you."

"That's exactly what Wiley told me. Then he goes looking for you all in an uproar, your wife says, and now he's dead."

"That don't prove anything. What were you talking to him about anyway?"

"The steroids."

"I sure was sorry your sister's boy got mixed up in that, but that still don't make any difference for Angel."

"If somebody at the Iron Body, namely Manly Richards, was selling them, it might make a big difference. I can't believe you knew about it and didn't even consider it."

He looked puzzled. "What are you talking about? We haven't even been over to get the boy's statement yet. Did you get hold of some bad turkey yesterday? Bad turkey will make you dream strange dreams. Bad turkey is what killed my granddaddy."

I refrained from telling him it was Wild Turkey that killed his granddaddy and related my conversation with Wiley.

"Damnation, why would Wiley say that? Vicki's boy didn't run into that tree until late yesterday."

"I don't know. My guess would be it has something to do with the reason he is lying here in the ditch."

He focused his eyes on mine. "How did you know about steroids on Wednesday anyway? You can get into more mess—I want to know where you heard it from."

"I might start remembering these things if you start looking for somebody to replace Angel in jail."

"Barbara, Edgar is going to be mighty unhappy if he has to come bail you out for obstructing justice."

"It's the bad turkey I ate yesterday. Bad turkey impairs your memory." I smiled innocently at J.C. I needed to talk to Bubba before J.C. did. If he got to him first I would never know anything else he found out.

"It'll take me until about two to get this wrapped up and then I'll expect you in my office. If you can't make it, I'll have Judge Wilson issue you an invitation to join Angel." Now was not the time to ask about the computer checks on Madame Zsa Zsa and Bunny.

J.C. turned to talk with one of the lab men who had walked over. I casually inched my way towards the body. I wanted to look at it, but, then again, I didn't. That's how Melissa is when we get to the scary part of a movie. She hides behind the chair and peeks out periodically to see if it's okay to look.

I glanced over in the direction of the body, prepared to look away in a hurry if need be. In my experience as a mother, I've been through several sets of facial stitches and an ear lobe hanging by a thread, but no bodies. The body was covered with a sheet, and I kept thinking any minute Wiley would sit up and yell, "Boo!"

As I turned to move away, a tall, skinny, somber-looking fellow who most certainly did some moonlighting at a funeral home moved the sheet. A bright orange

hunting vest flashed at me. Wiley's face showed no iden-
tifiable expression and gave off none of the macho aura
it had radiated only two days ago. His hunting vest was
torn near the left shoulder. The tear seemed to be the
only sign of trauma. The rest of the upper half of him
had sustained no gaping wounds or anything. It was evident the car had done more internal than external damage. Maybe that would be some small comfort to his
family. One of the young men from the truck brought
over a body bag. I found myself wishing I had talked to
Wiley a little longer at the station Wednesday. He had
lied about the steroids, and I wondered why. I thought
Bubba Pittman might know the answer.

I eased up the shoulder of the road some, past the
guys from the lab trying to make a cast of a tire track.
It didn't look very big, but I guess they needed to
cover everything. My destination was Wiley's black
Fiero parked up the road a few hundred feet. J.C.
stopped his conversation long enough to warn me of
the consequences of touching the car. I assured him I
was only window shopping.

Nothing about the car seemed that out of the ordi-
nary. A tape case lay open in the passenger seat, filled
with tapes of groups I had vaguely heard of and album
titles like *Dead Is Only a Word* and *You're So Hot I'm
Burning*. I tell you, I am not looking forward to my
children's adolescence.

I walked all around the car looking for something. I
wasn't sure what, but I was hoping for a sign. An obvious clue, the killer's handprint, I'd take anything I
could get. Wiley had been at the age where a clean car
is everything in life. Some men fixate at this stage and
are never able to move past it.

I walked around the car one more time hoping that, like Joshua and the Battle of Jericho, the walls would come tumbling down and a clue would be revealed.

Agent Bailey and J.C. were conferring again as I went past to the station wagon. I was going to have to work fast to get any information from Bubba before J.C. got a hold of him. I slung my brown leather purse across the console of the station wagon. Edgar says the FAA would make me check my purse with my luggage, it's so big. I carried everything, from wipes to reporter's pad to my handheld tape recorder in there. A good story waits for no reporter.

Agent Bailey walked away from J.C. He pulled his briefcase from his car and opened it on the hood. Looking through the contents, he shifted manila folders from one spot to another. He pulled out a black calendar book the size of a pocket diary and put it on the car hood. A black bag for a briefcase. *It was an interesting coincidence that he had a black bag,* I thought. Then I started counting up all the people I knew that owned black bags. Maybe it wasn't so interesting. I shut the door to the car, deciding I was going to ask him about Wednesday night. If J.C. weren't around, Agent Bailey might admit to me that he was in Martinsboro.

I was about ten feet from Agent Bailey when he must have found what he was looking for. He pulled a folded white paper from one of the pockets in the lid of his briefcase and walked off toward the medical examiner. His hand brushed the pocket calendar so that it opened flat on the car hood. I covered the rest of the ten feet and looked about to see if there was anything of interest to be seen in the briefcase. This man was organized. File folders occupied the bottom half of the briefcase. All of them had neat labels on the tabs and were in alphabetical order. I turned to go back to the car. He wasn't likely to admit his midnight trip in front of the medical examiner. An oblong piece of paper caught my eye. It was hanging from the edge of the pocket calendar. I recognized it as a charge slip for gas from the Dash Mart. Moving closer, I was almost able to see the date. I moved forward. November 26—that was Wednesday all right. Beside me a throat cleared.

"May I help you with something, Mrs. Upchurch?" Agent Bailey had circled around and come up behind me. He wasn't smiling.

"Not a thing, thank you. I was just leaving." There were altogether too many people who were having trouble with the truth. Two of them were dead. It would be nice for somebody to figure out what was going on before anyone else died.

10

Bubba Pittman *was harder to find* than I'd imagined. I drove by the Iron Body which was full of folks trying to lose all their Thanksgiving pounds in one shot. Then I went by the track, and I was about to give it up completely when I spotted his car at the Martinsboro Grill. A sporty blue Datsun with an ECU bumper sticker, it was as flashy and shiny as he was, and possibly as smart. (Good-looking men and good-looking Christmas trees are both dense, according to Alice. Bubba did nothing to dispute this theory.)

The Martinsboro Grill occupies a converted house that is painted a very unattractive shade of institutional green. The linoleum floors, which slant in towards the kitchen, used to be blue speckled, but most of the specks have worn off. The tables are all equipped with bottles of Texas Pete and shot glasses full of toothpicks. The booth seats are covered in green vinyl and the ladder-back chairs at the tables will pick your stockings. Of course, the grill isn't exactly the place to wear stockings. There is

a jukebox in the backroom that still has Charlie Rich
singing "Behind Closed Doors," and the grease they fry
the food in dates from the same period. Somehow, the
food tastes good and the place is always crowded.

Inside, the smell of cheeseburgers was enough to
make me forget that I'd sworn off food for good when
I left the dinner table the day before. Healthy eating is
a funny thing. I don't care what anybody says, everybody needs a little grease in their system. And I have
never seen a picture of one of those diet gurus in
which they look the least bit happy. They live to be
110, but they hate every minute of it.

Evidently, Bubba felt the same way about the issue.
He was in the back room listening to Randy Travis
singing "Forever and Ever, Amen" and getting ready to
dive into the biggest plate of cheeseburgers and onion
rings I'd ever seen. I tried not to look at them, though,
because I could feel my thighs growing already. It's
what I call the secondhand calorie phenomenon.
Secondhand calories are not a hot issue like secondhand
smoke, but the principle is the same. I know many people like myself whose blue jeans and skirts grow tighter
at the mere sight of fattening foods. I think the government should give a grant to a university to study it.

I slid across the green vinyl seat into the booth.
Bubba slowed his chewing momentarily.

"Bubba, something has come up which I hope you
can clarify for me." He kept chewing, picking up the
pace slightly. "You know that my sister's son Martin
Macauley is in the hospital as a result of his use of
steroids." I waved away the waitress, who was approach-
ing to take my order. "Nothing for me today, thanks."

Bubba swallowed. "No, Mrs. Upchurch, I had no idea.

Ma'am, you know I had nothing to do with that. I've seen him around the track, but that's all. He's a kid and—"

"Exactly, he is a kid, just eighteen. Whoever is responsible for this is in mighty big trouble." Every time I thought about Martin, I grew agitated. It seemed only last week, Vicki was calling to say what new word he'd learned, and here he was mixed up in this steroid business. The song on the jukebox ended and I lowered my voice. "Now, who was dealing for Manly?"

"Dag, Mrs. Upchurch, I don't know. I'm trying to make a football team, not become Columbo." He bit into a cheeseburger with a great snap, I imagine to show his righteous indignation.

"I suppose you know Wiley Bass is dead." He nodded yes. There probably wasn't anybody in town who didn't know that. It's a process Edgar calls "town osmosis."

I leaned in closer, getting a big whiff of onion rings in the process. "Did you know he was murdered?"

Bubba choked. As I got up, prepared to do the Heimlich maneuver, he recovered and I eased back onto the vinyl bench. He took a big swig of tea to clear his throat. "I thought it was a hit-and-run."

"Wednesday afternoon Wiley invented his own little story about what the Martinsboro police knew in connection with the Iron Body. Then I find out he went looking for J.C., but never found him. Instead he ended up dead on some back road."

Bubba looked puzzled.

"Tell the truth now, Bubba, Wiley knew something about this whole steroid issue. He was a muscular sort of guy, and I saw him reading a magazine with all these musclebound men on the front."

"What do you think he knew?" Bubba's face took on

a look of genuine interest. "You don't think anybody thinks I know the same thing?"

I couldn't resist a little melodrama. "Probably not or they would have come after you by now. But he did work out at the Iron Body, didn't he?"

Bubba nodded. "He was friendly with Manly, very friendly, now that I think about it. He was in and out of the office a lot. Manly never seemed to be concerned about him being a cop or anything."

"Think back. Did you ever see him with Manly and someone else together? Somebody who could be involved in the supply end of this?"

He pushed his brows together, trying to impress me with how hard he was thinking. "Nope, I can't think of a soul."

"Maybe it will come back to you." I wasn't going to bet the farm on it. "J.C. insists that I bring you over to answer a few questions." Bubba's face took on a greenish hue that sort of clashed with the booth seats.

"Great. That's all I need."

"You haven't done anything wrong, have you? As long as you weren't selling drugs, J.C. will most likely overlook your offense. Your use or possession of steroids or whatever it's classified in as the law. If you cooperate, and providing you haven't done anybody in or obstructed justice or any of his other little pet peeves."

He put down his cheeseburger.

"Chief Spivey might overlook it, but my mom sure as hell won't."

The hand that rocks the cradle rules the world.

"Okay, Bubba, here's the deal. If it comes to that, I'll help make sure that your mama understands that you were just a misguided young man in search of a career who is now going to go on the wagon, so to speak, and never do anything else to break his poor mama's heart. I'll do all that for a few answered questions and the promise if you think of anything else, you'll tell me first."

"I promise, but you think you can do any good? Sometimes my mom is real unreasonable."

I patted his hand. "I know, Bubba, it's something mothers catch from their children."

He grinned, and I decided maybe he wasn't such an awful waste of skin after all. He offered me an onion ring, so I guess the feeling was mutual.

"I'm trying to find out who his other partners were. Any ideas?"

He used a toothpick to get a piece of cheeseburger out of his bottom teeth. "Not a one. I really wasn't big pals with Manly, Mrs. Upchurch. I got my stuff from him, that's all."

"No idea of suppliers?"

"Nope." Somebody was going to have to know where Manly got his steroids.

"How about his wife? Did you know her?"

"Heard she was crazy, that's all."

"Crazy how? From who?"

"Peter York told me. She called and cussed at him all the time."

I could see we were the object of some speculation as we passed through to the front counter. Bubba paid his bill and picked up a pack of mints. No use smelling like onions on top of everything else, I suppose. As we headed for our cars I hoped that Edgar had been successful at finding the partners' names. This whole process was starting to give me a headache, and it wasn't even two o'clock.

° ° °

Things were bustling at the police station when we arrived. Everyone was busy, but not too busy to notice I had Bubba with me. Jackie swung around in her chair and raised her eyebrows at Ed when she thought I wasn't looking. Ed and Bubba talked football with all the intensity of a religious debate. And then just before Ed led us on into J. C.'s office, Bubba winked at Jackie, which was enough to send her back to her typing with a smile on her face. Ed appeared crestfallen when J. C. dismissed him and reminded him to close the door tight.

I was surprised to see Agent Bailey running his fingers over the surface of the purple-and-yellow golf ball on the credenza. Maybe J. C. was more serious about pursuing this than I'd thought.

"So it's a bowl for sure. How 'bout those Pirates?" J. C. grasped Bubba's hand in his.

"Excuse me?" Agent Bailey didn't get it.

J. C. turned to him. "This boy played for ECU. Offensive tight end, and damn fine one at that."

Bubba took all this in with the air of one who gets talked to this way all the time. I coughed loudly.

J. C. looked in my direction and pulled the corners of his smile down into a flat line. "Which is why I'm so concerned about this steroid business, son. You don't want to get yourself mixed up in all this mess." He motioned for Bubba to sit down. Bubba sat, putting his ankle up on his knee. His foot shook back and forth, and he gripped the arms of the chair like he was preparing for an airplane takeoff.

"Thank you for dropping by, Barbara. We'll be talking to you." J. C. opened the door.

"I'm staying." I started towards a chair.

"Not possible. If we need anything else from you"—
he grinned—"well, you know, don't call us, we'll call
you." I knew he wasn't bluffing and I knew I held an
ace he didn't know about. Bubba was going to cooperate with me because I was going to run interference
with his mom, so to speak.

"I'll wait right outside, if anyone needs me." I walked
out and took a seat in one of the chairs by Jackie.

"Too bad about Vicki's boy." Jackie fiddled with her
earring.

"Sure is. Thank the Lord he is going to be okay." I
shook my head. "What young love does to us."

"I heard there was more to it than that."

Small town, big news. "Yeah, well, we all have our
problems." I pulled my reporter's pad and started to
make notes. Jackie turned back to her typewriter. I'm
a list writer, and, when I don't forget my lists or lose
them, they help me keep organized. I started listing
suspects like groceries.

BUNNY RICHARDS
BELINDA BULLARD
MADAME ZSA ZSA
PARTNERS???
STEROID USERS???
BUBBA PITTMAN

Bubba was still a possibility, even if he was willing to
share his onion rings. I started to put down Martin,
but crossed his name off. I didn't think he could kill
anybody. (But then I wouldn't have thought he would
run that shiny blue Camaro into a tree.)

It was the third day since Angel's arrest, and I felt like I was making as much progress as the mythological guy that was assigned to roll the boulder up the hill in hell. Every time he gets it to the top, it rolls back down and he starts all over again. I dug through my pocketbook and found a Tylenol for my headache. I walked out into the hall, got a drink from the water fountain, and popped the pill in my mouth. I heard voices coming from the office. Bubba came out into the hall.

"How did it go?"

"Okay, I guess. Told them everything I told you. They said stick around. Like I'm going somewhere."

"Don't you feel better now having made a clean breast of things?" I moved past him towards the office door, shielding my pad where he was listed as a suspect.

He didn't answer the question, but pulled at my arm as I got even with him in the hall. "You haven't forgotten what you promised about my mom?"

"No, I haven't. You haven't forgotten what you promised me?"

"For sure," he gave me the thumbs-up sign and walked on towards the outside door.

I knocked on the door to J.C.'s office.

"Come in." I had the door open before J.C. finished his invitation. He crossed his arms. "I thought you left."

"My granddaddy would say, 'That's what you get for thinking.' "

"What's it gonna take to get you out of my hair?"

I didn't point out that with the rate he was going bald at that was using the term loosely. "I only want to know that you are pursuing this steroid connection. If it were your sister sitting in jail and your nephew in the hospital, you'd want to know." My voice cracked a little at the end of the sentence.

"I'm telling you what I'm gonna do. I'm gonna ask Agent Bailey to help with the investigation into the sale of steroids here in Martinsboro. I'm gonna have the medical examiner test Wiley's body for the presence of steroids. And I'm gonna throw your little *A double S* in jail if so much as one word leaks out about any of it until I make an official statement. You got all that down on your pad there?"

We were moving at last. I was relieved to hear the news of the SBI's involvement. The only problem was I didn't trust Agent Bailey. That did tend to complicate the issue.

"No need to get huffy about it; I'm only trying to help."

"That's what I'm saying. The only thing worse than you trying to help at this point is if the federal government tried to help me out. You know very well that we are stretched to the limit here and the sheriff's department is in worse shape. Those detectives have three hundred cases at one time and those are only felonies." His nose was going pink as his voice level rose. "This is a holiday weekend and I'm gonna have trouble keeping up with the regular round of domestic disturbances and DWIs, let alone getting a major investigation under way. You want miracles, go to church."

He was as stubborn as a mule. But, like a mule wearing blinders, he'd let me pull on him enough to make the turn down the steroid path, asking the medical examiner to do steroid testing and look for any signs of foul play more carefully than he might have otherwise. I could count on J.C. to plod along on this path, and hopefully not step in any hockey along the way. (I'm talking horse hockey here, not NHL.)

Agent Bailey was thrown into the role of peace-maker. "I'm sure Mrs. Upchurch knows we're doing all we can. I know she's going to let the matter rest in our hands now." He gave me a look that held the same steel as his voice.

As we were leaving his office, I pulled J. C. to the side. "Listen, one more thing. I think this Madame Zsa Zsa knew about Wiley's murder before you did. Something's fishy. I think Agent Bailey should run her and Bunny Richards through the computer."

J. C.'s eyes sort of bugged out and the vein in his neck became more prominent. "As your granddaddy would say, 'That's what you get for thinking.' Why don't you just get the town commissioners to create a supervisor's job for you over here at the department? Damnation, Barbara, you are not the only one around here with a brain. We are doing background checks on everybody."

He was ticked off because I knew about the steroids before he did.

I decided to go by the newspaper office and check the files for steroid stories. Mrs. Upchurch had packed me enough turkey and dressing to feed all the pilgrims on the Mayflower, so I didn't have to worry about what everyone was going to do for supper.

Alice was around her desk and out of her office before I'd had a chance to get in the door at the *News Herald*.

"Girl, Purdy wants to see you and Edgar's called several times asking to know did I expect you."

"Edgar probably wants to know what we're having for supper, but I don't know about Purdy. If he wants something on that story, he's going to be disappointed."

"He's saying that it's going around that Wiley was run over not by happening-to-be-there, but by selected-to-be-there. Says you know something about it."

"Now how does he know about Wiley?" And then, at the same time, we said, "Idaleen." Idaleen did not have enough to do over at the library.

Alice crossed her arms in front of her.

"She's been ringing here today as regular as church bells."

"I wish I could figure out what is going on."

Alice put a hand on my shoulder. "Go home, make Edgar take those kids out for pizza, and you climb in the bathtub with a Miller Lite for a good long soak. It'll come to you."

"Alice, you know good and well if I drink a Miller Lite in the bathtub Edgar and the kids will come home and find me drowned. Which wouldn't be such a bad idea; I've got so much stuff floating around in my brain and can't put any of it together to make any sense."

"Take your time, girl." Then she hummed a little of the beginning of "It Won't Be Long," an Andrae Crouch song. Alice had done the lead in the fall production of *Purlie* and, coming from her five-foot-three-inch frame, her voice was always a pleasant surprise.

"I don't have time." My voice rose a little above its natural pitch on the last word. It was then I realized there had been a steady stream of traffic to the water fountain since I'd come in. People were drinking as much water as camels before a journey across the desert.

Alice patted my arm and said, "Girl, haste makes waste.

I went on back to my corner of the office and called Edgar. He had the name of the lawyer who represented the corporation that owned the health club.

"You'll never guess who it is."

"I expect not. I don't know many lawyers in Raleigh."

"It's a local yokel. Guess who?"

"Edgar, hon, I don't want to guess who. I've been guessing who for three days now and it has gotten me nowhere."

"It's Arthur Talton and you don't have to jump all over me; I didn't get you into this." Now he was miffed. It was that kind of day.

Arthur Talton was a surprise. Maybe I could stop by his office on my way home.

"I know you didn't, and I appreciate the information. I'm going to try his office and then stop by the hospital to see Martin. I'll get supper together when I get home." That should help get me out of the doghouse.

No one answered the phone at Arthur Talton's office, so I headed over to the hospital and the big news that awaited me there. Looking up the information on steroids would have to wait. If I stayed at the office any longer, I was afraid Purdy would find me. I was not in the mood to answer questions when I still had so many myself.

11

There had been a breakthrough at the hospital. Unfortunately for Angel and Martin, it was for Misty Jane.

Vicki jumped from the chair beside Martin's bed when I pushed the door to the room open. She gave my shoulder a little squeeze and pushed the door shut. I nodded to Martin, whose ears were occupied with headphones from a Walkman. He grimaced. He wanted a visit from What's-her-name, not his Aunt Barbara. The hospital room was crowded with helium mylar balloons bearing greetings like, You're the Greatest and Get Well Soon.

"Barbara, you will never believe it. Dr. Merriwether was by earlier and took Misty Jane out for coffee. He even insisted she call him Joshua. Can you believe it?" And then I suppose she realized how that sounded and added. "I mean, after all, there are a lot of young ladies around he could take for coffee."

"That's great." I put my pocketbook on the bedside table amidst an assortment of music tapes for the Walkman and reached down to give Martin a hug. "And what's the word on our kamikaze cousin here?" Martin never missed a beat, his music knocking out any sound around him.

Vicki came up on the other side of the bed, stepping around his IV pole. "They are going to take the IV out later and he should be able to go home tomorrow as long as he rests well tonight." She patted his shoulder and reached behind him to plump a pillow. "There is a doctor in Raleigh Dr. Patterson would like him to see."

"I think J. C. might send someone over later to talk with him."

Vicki's hand smoothed the pillowcase. "I hope it's someone that knows what they're doing. The last thing Martin needs is excitement. You know, that—"

She smiled at Martin and motioned for me to follow her outside. I squeezed his arm to say good-bye and waved as I picked up my pocketbook to follow his mother out the door.

As soon as the wooden door had swung shut, Vicki moaned. "That girl has been here twice. She doesn't want to break up with Martin after all." Vicki's face puffed up like a storm cloud. "The little, oh, the little hussy. It isn't like she hasn't done enough damage already." Her hands moved around one another in constant motion.

"It will work out, Vicki. I know it's aggravating. But, you know, if you carry on about her, that will only make Martin hang on to her more. Everything will work out in its own good time." This is advice I give when it is not my children.

"I suppose you're right. Why, look at Misty Jane,

starting on the romantic adventure of her life." Vicki's
eyes were bright with anticipation. I was not in the
mood for bridal discussions. I left before my dark
mood could prick the balloon of her excitement. Vicki
had enough problems without me bringing her down.

Less than an hour later, I was sitting at the supper
table taking part in that almost extinct custom, the
family meal. "Is Misty Jane getting married?" Melissa
asked after we had blessed the leftover turkey. Edgar
had especially requested that the Lord see to it that
this was the last meal from this turkey.

"I don't want a repeat of the five loaves and three
fishes," he said when I shot him a look. I turned to
Melissa and smiled.

"Someday, she'll get married, but probably not any-
time soon." I hadn't realized the children had over-
heard my discussion with Edgar about Dr.
Merriwether and Misty Jane. They can't hear me tell
them to clean their rooms from three feet away, but
information they don't need to know they can hear
from one end of the house to the other.

Then, as an afterthought, I added, "Don't ask her
about it, though. She's sort of, well, sensitive on the
subject of marriage right now."

"And how!" said Becky, rolling her eyes.

I folded my hands under my chin and sent a steady
gaze in her direction. She got busy on her mashed
potatoes.

Jason asked me, "When is Aunt Angel going to get
out of jail?"

I don't know why we don't ever play twenty questions about Edgar's family; after all, they have had a
few scandals in the last decade.

All three children turned their faces toward me. I was reminded again that motherhood brings no guaranties of being able to protect your children from the world and its harsh reality. It starts when they're little and fall over one of their toys. They get up off the floor and give you a look that says, "How could you have possibly let me fall?" That progresses, slowly but surely, to moments like now.

I put my fork down. I was losing my appetite anyway.

"Well, Aunt Angel sort of got involved with the wrong group of people and now she has gotten herself in a serious mess which she could have avoided if she had different friends. It looks like Martin might have the same problem." Having their full attention, I couldn't resist a little moralizing. "Which only goes to show how carefully you need to pick your friends."

In an involuntary teenage reflex, Becky's eyes rolled again. A mom's advice to a teenager does to their eyes what the doctor's hammer does to their knees.

Ignoring her, I continued. "We all hope and pray that the mistake is quickly recognized and she gets out of jail soon."

Jason shook his head. "Drew says Aunt Angel is going to fry. I kicked him right in his privates when he said it."

Edgar spoke up. "Your Aunt Angel is going to be fine. A lot of people are working very hard to find out what really happened, including your mom. That means a lot of pizza and fast food for us." He smiled. "Think you can stand the sacrifice?"

The children smiled back at their dad. Edgar's menu suited them fine. Edgar doesn't cook, and the oldest two children still swear that they were forced to eat Raisin Bran three meals a day when I was in the hospital having Jason.

Melissa's smile changed to a frown and she began to cry. The most dramatic of our three children, Melissa didn't cry a few sniffles into her napkin, but loud, racking sobs across the table, with her arms outstretched. High drama is a way of life for Melissa. She's going to make a great Baptist.

I patted her hand. "Aunt Angel and Martin will be okay."

She sobbed louder. "Not that, the note from my teacher. It's because we were passing notes in class. It's just like you said—it wasn't my fault at all. It was my friends, Christy Adams and Julie Muller."

"Is that right?" I asked her feeling the color come back to my face again and the vein in my neck beginning to pound. I frowned across the table at her, though I have to admit I was secretly relieved to be back to some of the more mundane issues of life.

"I guess Aunt Angel and I are kindred spirits," she wailed clasping her hands together in a melodramatic fashion. We had watched the *Anne of Green Gables* videos earlier in the month and Melissa was quite taken with Anne. She used many of the phrases from the movie when she talked.

"I'm not sure I'd go that far. I'm surprised Miss Hudson was upset enough over your notes to want a conference. What was in them?"

Melissa twisted the corner of her mouth. "Well, she was confused; she thought there were some test answers on them. But not really. She didn't see—"

I held up my hand. "This is obviously a subject you

and I need to discuss privately. Unless your dad would care to do the honors?"

Edgar shook his head. "I'm never a man to mess with a good plan. Sounds like a great plan to me."

Becky took hold of Melissa's hand and turned over her palm. "I see months of being grounded stretching out before you." Melissa jerked her hand away and stomped off up the stairs.

Becky grinned. "How about that? Am I psychic or what? Just like Madame Zsa Zsa."

Saturday I called in all my favors from other mothers on Jason and Melissa's basketball teams to get the kids to practice. Becky hibernated upstairs in her room, coming downstairs only long enough to grab some cheese danish and an egg she was going to use to wash her hair. I didn't realize that was popular again.

I called Arthur Talton's home number and got an answering machine. I left a message asking him to call me at home if he got in before Monday. Edgar had gone hunting early in the morning, but agreed before he left to pick up Jason and Melissa at ball practice.

"Becky, I'm going to the hospital to see Martin. Don't go out until your dad gets here. Write down the messages. I always miss one or two if you try to remember them." Becky stood at the top of the stairs, head wrapped in a red towel, mouth full of hair paraphernalia, and grunted her acknowledgement of these instructions, which is not the same thing at all as agreeing to them.

Vicki met me at the door of Martin's room. "Martin is going home today. Isn't that great news?"

Martin sat on the edge of the bed wearing a sweat-shirt and jeans. His face was an assortment of colors.

"That is great news!"

Martin gave me a halfhearted smile. "Maybe I'll get some decent food anyway."

"He has already told me what he wants to eat for the next three days." Vicki was packing Martin's things. She pushed a plastic hospital pitcher down into a bag as she talked.

"Did J. C. send somebody by to see you?"

Without looking up, Vicki answered, "J. C.'s going to send somebody out to the house, but Agent Bailey came by earlier. Took his own personal time to come over here and talk to Martin."

I wished this impressed me as much as it did Vicki.

"What did you tell him, Martin?"

Martin studied a spot on the sheet. "I told him I bought the stuff from a football player, Mike Hudgins. He wrote his name down. I'm going to be in so much trouble."

Mike Hudgins's name didn't sound familiar. "Martin, this would have come out sooner or later. There is no way you can keep that kind of information to yourself just so you can be popular." He didn't lift his head. "You could be prosecuted for withholding that kind of infor-mation."

Vicki's head came up. "Barbara, don't go telling him that." The handle of the pitcher hung on the outside of the bag. Vicki snatched at it. "He is not a common criminal."

"Vicki, I didn't say he was. I only want him to under-stand he was not in any kind of bargaining position."

She pulled the bag shut, having succeeded in stuffing

the pitcher inside. "Sometimes, Barbara, there are more important things than sticking your nose into everything and having to know it all. I don't know when you're going to wake up."

I suppressed the urge to tell her ignoring things and having coffee was not the best plan either. None of us was doing well with all of this. First Angel, then Martin. There had to be some way of unraveling all this information to come up with some answers. I was pulling the wrong string in the cloth. If I could only find the right one the whole thing would unravel. My self-esteem was suffering in the meantime.

Joshua Merriwether came by the door then. He was sporting his best bedside manner. Vicki ran a hand over her skirt and checked her hair in the mirror over the sink. I used his entrance as an excuse to leave. Vicki waved to me like a rider on a parade float as I left.

I checked my pocketbook for the address of Manly's house in High Cotton Estates. I took the back way into Martinsboro, the wide-open fields and barns along the way calming me after Vicki's exposé on my shortcomings. I passed a hunter's Chevy Blazer parked along the roadside and thought of Edgar. I hoped he remembered what time the children got home from practice. Becky was old enough to look after everyone, but usually there was a fight. I got to mediate when I returned home, so I didn't like to leave them for very long. It's tough being the one in charge all the time. The rule maker, the Medusa, the woman to answer to. When they were small, you could redirect their behavior or give them a nap, or if worst came to worst, pick them up and move them to where you wanted them. Bigger is different. Somewhere along the way, I found myself reading magazine articles with titles like "Get the Household Cooperation that You Need" and "Helping Your Mate to Reap the Joys of Shared Parenting." To borrow a line from Shakespeare, back in "my salad days when I was green in judgment," I thought all of this would come naturally. Children would cooperate, husband would chip in, we'd all ride off together on the prince's white stallion—or at least climb mountains wearing matching outfits—singing "The Sound of Music."

I do clip all the articles I can find on sensitive men. I underline the parts about bonding and nurturing and all. Edgar uses them to cover the back steps when he cleans fish. Edgar is a chauvinist by accident. The world was set up for him to get to be somebody apart from being the dad, and so he thought that it worked the same for me.

He sees it a little now. He has a glimmer of the reality that when one of us gets up on Saturday morning and wants to go to the hardware store, he goes. When the other one gets up on Saturday morning and wants to go to the grocery store, she has to make sure all the children are arranged.

Taking the reporter's job helped. People see me again, even if only for a moment, as somebody besides the mom, the wife, the hostess promoting her husband's mill career by giving the Christmas open house, talking crafts and bows with the mill wives. That was one of the reasons I couldn't let this steroid stuff alone. I'm more than the sum of wife, mother, rulemaker, hostess, daughter, sister.

Trees came in patterns beside the road. A string of similarly-sized maples covered in late-changing red leaves heralded my arrival at High Cotton Estates. I turned right past the brick sign with ornamental cabbage and pansies planted in front. My red station wagon was inconspicuous in the family-oriented subdivision. I found the address, a two-story, Williamsburg-type house with taupe shutters and crossbars forming window panes. I parked several blocks down the street. Noting the community watch plates on all the mailboxes, I hoped everyone thought I was somebody else's Thanksgiving company.

I walked around to the back of the house. The deck was small, with a Weber grill on one side and brown leaves piled in the corners against the latticework and in front of the back door. The door was half glass, and through it I could see the empty kitchen. A note taped to the back read "Clean all carpets except the bedrooms upstairs." I guess the rental people were trying to get the house ready to be shown again. I hoped that didn't mean all of Manly's stuff was gone. I tried the knob. It turned in my hand. I pushed gently, trying to make as little noise as possible, which wasn't easy with all those leaves in front of the door. I stepped into the kitchen.

"Anybody home?"

No answer. Maybe I would peek around to see if there were any possible clues that the police had missed. Couldn't hurt anything.

I was noting Manly's lack of matching dishes when I heard the floor in the next room creak. Not a good sign. I eased my hand down from the cupboard door and looked about the counter for a suitable weapon. A blender wouldn't work. All the idiots in this country that have a handgun and where is one when you need it? Above the sink hung a rack of knives. I would have to really stretch to reach them.

Too late. Out of the corner of my eye, I saw a form

move into the kitchen. I lunged for the knives and screamed. The form screamed back.

I turned with my hand grabbing at the air around the handle of a serrated knife to find Madame Zsa Zsa, a yellow caftan billowing around her, with her arms waving and her mouth open wide. I think I saw her tonsils.

"What are you doing here?" I demanded when I could breathe well enough to talk.

"My dear, I could ask you the same thing."

"And I'll be asking you both." In the doorway stood Bunny Richards. Her hair was now one complete honey shade and she was dressed in a black form-fitting sheath. Her heels were so high that not only could I not have balanced myself on them, I would have gotten a nose bleed from wearing them.

Old home week and no one had brought any food. I spoke first. "I thought that there might be something here that the police overlooked. The door was open, so I came on in."

Bunny seemed to accept this, and she and I both turned to Madame Zsa Zsa.

She stepped towards Bunny. "Oh, you must be the widow. Honey, I feel so much for your loss." Bunny didn't move. "I had given the late Mr. Richards some crystals to keep and I'm here trying to locate it. Crystals are very powerful objects; they can unlock the secrets of the universe."

Maybe, maybe not.

Bunny stepped into the kitchen. "You're not Manly's regular type."

Madame Zsa Zsa laughed, a tinkling sound that closely resembled her jewelry banging together. "No, I was Manly's adviser on his spiritual affairs."

"Hon, if they were anything like the rest, I don't know how you kept up with it all."

"Bunny, you told Vicki and me the other day you didn't know anything about this house. I'm sort of surprised to see you here myself." I studied Bunny's face to see her reaction. It was smooth, with no hint of hesitation.

"I didn't until you told me about it. As the deceased Mr. Richards's widow, all of this stuff belongs to me."

Madame Zsa Zsa moved towards the kitchen door. "I'm afraid I must be going. I've got several readings to do this afternoon and I like to take a nap and be rested before I start."

Bunny stepped to the side to let Madame Zsa Zsa past. "So did you find those crystals?"

"What? Oh, no, fortune was not smiling on me." Madame Zsa Zsa held up two empty palms. "If you find them, you will save them? Let me give you a card to get in touch." The madame pulled a printed business card from a shapeless tapestry sack she carried on her shoulder.

Bunny took the card. "Sure, what do I want with a bunch of rocks?"

The madame closed her eyes and seemed to sway. Reflex caused me to jump towards her, but she remained on her feet. Her eyes remained closed. "You are with child?"

I felt a momentary surge of panic. I had given the baby bed away last month, an action, people joked, that would result in the conception of another baby. The madame opened her eyes and looked at Bunny. My shoulders relaxed.

Bunny scrutinized the psychic as if she had appeared out of thin air. "Who says so?"

Madame Zsa Zsa reached back from the doorway and patted Bunny's arm. "I sense these things. It will be a happy occasion for you. You must come some time and let me read for you. My number is on the card. For you, I would charge only the smallest of fees."

Then she was gone. I realized I was still holding the serrated knife and turned to place it in the holder by the window. On the sidewalk, out of the view of the back door, Madame Zsa Zsa removed something from her pocket and put it in her bag. She might not have found her crystals, but she found something else she wanted.

I turned back to Bunny. "Congratulations. Did Manly know he was going to be a father?"

"No. Look, I've got a lot to do here. You're welcome to look through the house, but get on with it. I've got someone coming to help me decide what of this junk is worth selling."

The tour of the house was disappointing. No clues to the partners and no notepads with pages ripped off so I could rub a pencil across to reveal the phone number of the steroid connection. The only thing I discovered in my tour of the house was Manly's complete lack of taste. The whole place was furnished in early bachelor, a cross between the Elvis Presley school of decorating and pictures of those ads for honeymoon hotels in the Poconos.

Bunny had been puttering around, looking ever the expectant mother in her black sheath and high heels. She seemed glad when I moved towards the door. She didn't push me out, but it was close.

I walked past a blue Ford pickup truck in the driveway that Bunny must have driven to haul away her prizes. It was a good hike back the several blocks to where I had left the car. By the time I turned around and drove back by Manly's house, a long-haired young man was pulling Bunny's teal Trans Am into the driveway. Could this be the daddy? I tried to slow down enough to get a good look, but the baseball cap pulled down low over his forehead made it impossible to tell much about him.

Everybody was hiding something. It might not be such a bad thing to be psychic; I might be able to figure out what each one of them didn't want me to know.

When I got back to the house, the children greeted me at the door. "Daddy showed us the farm we're going to buy and the barn where we can keep our horse and everything. Isn't that great?"

Their daddy stood behind them, disclaiming as fast as he could. "Now, guys, I said maybe. There's a lot we've got to work out."

I moved past them towards the kitchen. "For instance, a new wife for you, Dad." I sat down at the kitchen table.

"Please, Mom, please. It'll be so cool." Jason stood in front of me. Melissa was beside him. "We'll do everything. Clean the house, feed the horse. Take care of the puppies when they're born. Rake the yard."

"What puppies? And let me remind you, it took me one complete Saturday's worth of constant reminding to get the backyard raked. Raking our backyard doesn't come close to the work involved on a farm. I'd have to see a lot more effort around here before I'd even think of moving to a farm."

I shot their father a meaningful look.

Melissa smiled. "Dad says we'll have redbone coonhound puppies, Mom. Please, pretty please. We'll make money when we sell the puppies."

Edgar was backtracking fast. "Okay, guys, leave your mom alone. We'll talk about this a little later."

"Ten, fifteen years is a good time frame." I stretched my legs out in front of me. Edgar shooed the children from the kitchen. He came over and rubbed my shoulders.

"So what did you find out today?"

"Too late to ask that. You make me so mad. Edgar, you know that I can't possibly think about one more thing and so you take the kids out and start talking 'Green Acres' with them. You know that's not fair."

"Well, I was only trying to keep them out of your way so you could get this thing with your sister taken care of and we could get on with our lives." His hands stopped their kneading. "Tell you what, we've all had a long day, what do you say we go out to dinner tonight?"

The man was no dummy.

Dinner, baths, and checking church clothes for cleanliness occupied the rest of the evening. I took some comfort in the regular routine of life. The children watched a Christmas special with their dad. I went to bed and was asleep by nine o'clock.

The church was full on Sunday. The poinsettias had already been set out in the sanctuary and added a splash of red all around the pulpit. Mann's Chapel Baptist was a simple church where I had worshiped for years. Ministers came and ministers left, but I could always walk into that simple sanctuary with its stained wood and white walls and find some peace.

People came by and squeezed my arm. "We're praying for you," they would say. In the buzz before morning announcements, I heard Angel and Martin's names more than once. Baptists are not known for their reverence in the sanctuary. Organ music aside, social time lasts right up until the minister starts speaking. One minute you're discussing the details of who Pinky Jackson left his wife for and the next you are bowing your head in prayer, your sentence clipped in the middle or hurriedly mouthed to the lip reader behind you.

Of course, our children are still not quite old enough for me to hear much of the sermon. Becky sits with the other middle school children, and I have to keep giving her that don't-do-that-again-or-you'll-wish-you-hadn't look.

I suppose the first time you can really concentrate on what the minister is saying, you're too old for it to do you much good anyway. Who says God doesn't have a sense of humor?

12

Arthur Talton's secretary answered the phone on Monday. She put me on hold after I told her my business. I cleaned away the last remains of breakfast, giving the Berry Berry Kix that remained in Jason's bowl to the dog and listening to Lite 96 playing in my ear while I waited. I hummed two choruses of "My Girl" before she returned. In a crisp voice, heavy with English accent, she explained that Mr. Talton's schedule was "tight." I couldn't imagine how it could be any tighter than her voice.

"He has appointments all day."

That gave me enough information to know it was worth a trip to the office. I looked around the house for the match to my blue pump, wondering if in the wake of Edgar and the children leaving for the day I could get the governor to declare the house a disaster area and get us some relief. It took a full ten minutes for me to find the shoe in the hall closet behind the vacuum and under Jason's raincoat, which was thrown down on the floor of the closet. I wore a navy jacket over a simple, red, cotton-knit dress with a flared skirt and an expandable waistline, trying for a neat but not imposing look. Sometimes you get more information if people, particularly men people, think your elevator doesn't go all the way to the top floor.

Arthur Talton's office was in an old hotel downtown that his daddy owned and which he had converted into an office complex, complete with fox hunters in various stages of the hunt on the wall and a mural of the blind figure of Justice with the scales in her hands.

Justice had not been blind in the case of Arthur's daddy, Monroe Talton. Justice had been bought. Monroe Talton had made his money in many illegal activities, not limited to moonshine, prostitution, cock fights, and the like. Monroe made Weekie John, an Erwin bootlegger, look like he was running a lemonade stand.

Families like the Taltons always produce at least one lawyer because they need them so badly. Arthur had gone off to Texas for a few years, practicing as an attorney for a large oil company. He had come back a short time before his daddy died with the uncanny ability to distance himself from his daddy's more shady activities. His inheritance was large, and a lot of that moonshine money now went to support political candidates who were continuing in spirit some of Monroe Talton's activities, taking from the poor to give to the rich.

The secretary I had spoken to earlier sat at a large mahogany desk with a nameplate on one side which read SYLVIA PERKINS. Sylvia Perkins had a regal manner with which she surveyed the room and myself. This air made her appear to be one of the queen's distant relatives. Either she didn't like the English climate or all the secretarial positions at the palace were full. Despite all this, she was a pretty woman in a meticulous sort of way, with blonde hair and a soft winter-white sweater dress with a purple paisley scarf and purple heels. The sweater dress was the only thing soft about her. She got more of an attitude when I told her who I was and repeated her earlier statement about Arthur's schedule in a loud voice that indicated she thought I was possibly deaf or had been a slow-witted student in school.

"I understand what a busy man Mr. Talton is. That is why I'll be brief."

She pushed her lips in and out. "I'll call Mr. Lyles, who is Mr. Talton's assistant."

I shook my head. "I'll still want to speak to Mr. Talton, and I'm afraid I won't leave until I do."

The assistant would most likely do, but this had become a matter of principle now. My tragic flaw. I have been known on occasion to cut off my nose to spite my face. Besides, for a man with a day full of appointments, Arthur Talton had a very empty office.

"As I said earlier, it's about the Iron Body Health Club. Mr. Talton is listed on the incorporation papers."

She tapped her pink manicured nails on the desk and glared at me. I involuntarily moved my unpolished nails behind my back, where she couldn't see them.

"I think that you are missing the point. I'm doing Mr. Talton a favor. I could just give all this to Purdy, and he'd have to wait for the paper to come out to read about it all."

Her glare became more hostile, though that seemed

impossible. I sensed that that was a good time to go sit and catch up on some magazine reading. None of the magazines looked that inviting, but I settled on a recent *Time* and began to read, watching Ms. Perkins go through the door behind her. She returned in a minute, and I had time to finish an article on Serbia and Bosnia before Arthur Talton appeared. Arthur and I knew each other slightly from attending various Chamber of Commerce activities together.

Arthur came through the door, filling it with his massive form. He was consistent: big man, big inheritance. He had salt-and-pepper hair that was cut and styled in a pompadour and a suit that was obviously tailored to slim his bulk. He extended his arm and before I could move out of the way had hugged me to him.

"Barbara, what a pleasant surprise. I couldn't believe it when Sylvia told me you were out here."

"I don't think Sylvia could quite believe it either." I pushed myself away from the expensive silk of his suit.

At my comment, Arthur threw his head back and laughed. "Sylvia is a damn fine secretary and she does her best to minimize my interruptions."

Arthur ushered me into his office; an antique desk and furnishings combined with old photographs in gilt frames had the striking effect of making you feel like you had entered a different era. No pictures of Justice in here; she was nice to look at, but you wouldn't want to live with her. Unlike J.C., Arthur was a Duke fan, and there were a few mementos to celebrate this year's NCAA basketball championship, including a signed picture of Arthur with Christian Laettner and Bobby Hurley. Arthur had gotten an undergraduate degree from Duke as well as his J.D. from the Duke law

school. In this part of the country we call Duke fans
"Dookies," which coincidentally is the name we used
as children for what the dog does in piles in the yard.

We exchanged pleasantries about the coming basketball season and Arthur predicted a second NCAA
basketball championship for his team. I could only
hope that the University of North Carolina Tarheels
would deprive them of the chance.

"Arthur, I need information on the partners in the
health club. I'm trying to get all the facts that I can to
try and help Angel out of this mess. Nobody knows
who the partners are, but you're listed on the incorporation papers—"

He interrupted. "Barbara, I don't really think information about the partners is going to help Angel out
and it's my job to protect my clients from negative
publicity. As far as the use and sale of illegal sub-
stances, I can assure you my clients have no connection to those activities. Edgar needs to keep an eye on
you before you get hurt." His face had changed as he
spoke; it lost the soft, smiley look, and now his mouth
looked thin and set.

"Edgar knows I'm perfectly capable of looking after
myself."

"I don't know about that, Barbara. You could mess
with the wrong person. As I tell my daughters all the
time, girls are not just long-haired boys."

He laughed at what he thought was his own clever-
ness. I prayed his daughters would give all his money
to NOW when they inherited it. Another pedestal to
climb onto—it could wear a "girl" out. Arthur's ideas
about women coincided nicely with the antique decor
of his office. Arthur would never admit to it, but he

didn't like women. He had never passed the stage that Jason was in now.

"Well, J.C. is a boy and I suppose I could talk fast enough to get a subpoena of the records." I emphasized the word *boy*.

His face was all lines now. "I will hold you personally responsible if any of my clients have any negative publicity from this. They are decent citizens who wish to remain quiet investors." On the word investors, Arthur rose from his chair.

Never one to like to look up to men with Arthur's attitude, I rose, too. "If they are decent citizens, they won't have a thing to worry about."

I left Arthur's office with the names and phone numbers of the Iron Body partners.

13

No doubt the minute I left his office Arthur was on the phone to his clients. Since I couldn't surprise them, I decided I might as well let them stew in the knowledge of their impending exposure for a little while. Now that I knew who they were, they certainly weren't going anywhere. If I called them from the office beforehand, they might sweat even more.

The office was bustling after the weekend. Velena Moore was in getting her religious column ready, and both Jay and Mitchell were busy at their computer stations. Mitchell looked up.

"I believe Purdy is looking for you." He managed to lift his nose a notch at the end of the sentence.

"I'm going to miss him then because Alice says he has gone over to the mayor's prayer luncheon. I hate it, but it can't be helped."

Jay turned from his computer. "Have you found out anything important yet? I heard there is a drug connection involved." He hesitated. "Sorry about your nephew."

"He's in my prayers," Velena echoed Jay's sentiment. Even Mitchell inclined his head to indicate some sort of sympathy.

"Nobody is sure of much right now. It looks like it's only going to get more complicated."

Mitchell sniffed loudly and turned back to the story he was working on, a lead-in to a series we are running on the congressional bank scandal. If I'd known you didn't have to balance your checkbook to be in Congress, I might have considered a career in politics myself.

Jay continued, "I made a few calls on the stories you asked me to help you on. Do you want to talk about them now or wait until later?"

"Let's do it and get it over with."

"On this federal grant to the schools story, I had a little trouble reading your notes." Jay poked my arm. "The way you write you really should have been a doctor, Barbara."

From Mitchell, "I think Egyptian hieroglyphics writer is a more likely choice."

My signature is a *B* with a squiggle after it and a *U* with a flat line ending in a loop and a hump. The girl at the dry cleaners has asked me if my bank would accept my check like that, and I frequently end up showing clerks at mall stores that my driver's license was signed in the exact same style.

Jay and I had discussed the stories for about fifteen minutes when Alice's voice came through the phone intercom. "Barbara, there is a man on the phone. Says his name is Mordecai Bethune. Says you know why he's calling. Since you know so much, tell me, is this the Mordecai Bethune?"

The Right Reverend Mordecai Bethune was the executive secretary of the CHOOSE GOD denomination. CHOOSE GOD is an acronym for Church Holy of the Omnipotent Sacred Eternal God. CHOOSE GOD is one of those denominations/organizations that believes in the richness of the Christian life, particularly for the denomination's hierarchy. You could give cash or you could choose God through your Visa or MasterCard.

"One and the same, I'm sure."

"I thought so, girl. I was wanting to zip my pocketbook up just listening to him talk on the phone."

At this, Velena Moore turned around. "I had no idea you knew the Right Reverend Bethune, Barbara. That man is a saint of God, a pillar of this community, and a true ambassador for Christ."

Velena seemed unaware of the reverend's other calling. Mordecai Bethune and his colleague, the Reverend James Creech, were the silent partners in the Iron Body Health Club. Judging from the amount of time the reverend took to find me, he wasn't in a stew, he was much closer to a full boil.

Mitchell, Jay, and Velena all looked my way as I picked up the phone.

"This is Barbara Upchurch."

"Mrs. Upchurch, this is Reverend Mordecai Bethune. I understand from my attorney that you would like to talk with me."

I had to keep my end of the conversation short. "That's right."

"Well, I'm not one to beat around the bush about these things."

No, I thought, *that's why God made attorneys*.

The voice continued. "What if you came by some time this afternoon, say one o'clock, and we will get this misunderstanding all cleared up?"

"Will Reverend Creech be there?"

"Uh-huh, he'll be here. He's as anxious as I am to get this mess—misunderstanding—cleaned up."

"Great."

"We will see you here at my office at one then."

"Unless you'd rather gather at the river."

The reverend clicked the phone without so much as a snicker. The man had no sense of humor.

Mitchell and Jay were staring intently at me, but I had no desire for anyone to know what was happening until I had been able to have a little conversation with the reverends.

At about the time Mitchell opened his mouth, the intercom buzzed again. Alice's voice danced with agitation. "Barbara, I need you to get your little hiney on up here. We got some serious shh—stuff going down. So you make like the 'Price Is Right' folks and come on down."

"On my way." I grabbed my purse and pad and was almost out the door when I realized some explanation was better than no explanation. "Have I mentioned to y'all that Angel has been thinking about becoming a missionary?" I headed through the door as Mitchell said something like "To where? Central Prison?" Velena clapped her hands and said, "Praise the Lord!"

Alice was standing behind her desk with her hand on her hip. Every piece of Alice's anatomy was thrown full force into what she did. She could speak more with her hand on her hip than some people could speak in a month. Clothes can say who you are or who you are not. Alice's said, "This is me. Take it or leave it." The outfit she wore, a gauzy print skirt and body suit with flowing overblouse, added to her mystique.

"Okay, girl, I will tell you what I know, which is, by the way, important to you. *If* you tell me straight why the right reverend, keeper of the cash flow, would be calling you."

"Alice, you know I don't have time for this. Any minute Purdy may come walking through the door."

She looked at her watch. "According to my calculations, they are just now starting the fried chicken. Haven't even touched the dessert or the praying, except to bless the food, of course. We've got time. Besides, it's not like I'm going to be broadcasting this news of yours to anyone. And the last thing I want to have happen is for you to get killed or brainwashed by some man who is way out there."

She frowned at me and made a gesture up and out with her hands like you made when you were a blooming flower in the second grade play. "You know the right reverend is *way* out there."

She was right, of course. About the reverend as well the fact that she could keep a secret. I checked around to make sure there were no other ears in the reception area around Purdy's office.

"The Reverend Bethune and his colleague, the Reverend James Creech, are the principal stockholders in the company which is the principal stockholder in the Iron Body Health Club."

"Oowee, give 'til it hurts. Amen."

"I'm going out to meet with the reverends at one. What was it that you needed to tell me?"

"Mr. Arthur Talton has called up Mr. Purdy Newsome all in a huff and when I asked him what was the call in reference to, he said Ms. Barbara Upchurch. I put it at the bottom of the messages, but I think you better get going before Purdy gets back and chews on you for his afternoon snack."

I pulled on my coat. "That's the truth. If I could get this thing worked out and have a story, he would care less what Arthur Talton thinks of me. Nothing gets in the way of a good story for Purdy."

"Amen, sister, you are preaching to the choir. Don't I know how many late nights I've spent here."

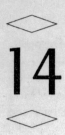

14

The offices of CHOOSE GOD occupied a thirty-acre campus and compound south of Dunn. The campus contained the national headquarters of the denomination, the seminary, the undergraduate and graduate schools of CHOOSE GOD University, and the television studios from which the bright star of the network, Mordecai Bethune, was featured in the LTP Club (Loud the Praise). James Creech ministered to the congregation of the CHOOSE GOD Cathedral every Sunday morning.

Mordecai and James, like the wise man in the vacation Bible school song, did not build their house upon the sand. And like the three pigs in the nursery tale, they realized brick was best. Colonial-style brick buildings were everywhere you looked. Even the cathedral and the guardhouse at the main gate were built as if the redcoats were coming any minute.

Apart from the campus, but included in the thirty-acre

complex, was a plantation house that had been restored
to its original glory. This was the reverends' idea of a
tourist trap. CHOOSE GOD billboards rivaled those
of South of the Border on Interstate 95. The CHOOSE
GOD billboards had catchy little slogans like:

FREE WATER

FREE AIR

FREE SALVATION

CHOOSE GOD sponsored a Christmas choral
evening at the plantation house with music and mulled
cider every year. It was a well-orchestrated event that I
often covered for the *News Herald.* Somehow, as I
drove through the complex filled with various shapes
and sizes of people, I couldn't get over the feeling that
even the way groups of people walked, and their desti-
nations, were orchestrated.

The offices of Mordecai Bethune were in the very
heart of the campus in an imposing building, mod-
eled along the lines of the House of Government at
Williamsburg.

The interior held a foyer with a marbled floor and
staircase. The staircase had a shiny brass banister that
wound its way up to the open area at the top of the
stairs. The old prom theme "Stairway to Heaven"
came from some dark corner of my mind, where,
thank the Lord, it had stayed for eighteen years. I
could imagine Jason and Melissa sliding down the banister with their hands in the air and their mouths open.
Becky is way too dignified for that these days.

This kind of stairway and the plantation house were
enough to perpetuate the image many Yankees who

passed down 95 on their way to Florida have of the South; we are mint julep–drinking dull wits whose minds have been so slowed by the sun that we need Northerners to come down and supervise us.

That's how images are, overdone. Nobody ever writes about the regular folks. About women like my grandmother, who spent her life not worrying about her corset stays or drunk at the honky tonk, but raising seven children, burying two more, and working in the heat of the denim mill in Erwin, going home at night with lint clinging to her clothes and skin. A woman whose voice you could hear singing as you came up the church steps long before you ever saw her, who left a legacy of love that will make the world a better place. That is not interesting. No one wants to hear about regular.

Instead, they write about men like my great-grandfather, her daddy. Widowed in his sixties, he promptly married a woman who was passing through town from some unspecified origin. He met her at a local café. She was in her thirties, though she appeared older according to family sources. At night she would call to him from the bedroom, "Mr. Edwards, I'm waiting for you to come to bed." The marriage lasted three months, whereupon it is agreed by the same family sources that he decided he felt more his age than he'd originally thought. He bought his new bride a bus ticket for a destination in the North, and she was never heard from again.

The receptionist's desk sat at the foot of the stairs. The decor surrounding her was designed to give the feeling of a home—big ferns and a colonial-period sofa and chairs formed a sitting area to her right, large mirrors and formal portraits adorned the walls. Among the painted faces, I recognized Mordecai and James looking down upon the room with benevolent smiles.

The young woman behind the reception desk was blonde and busty, though conservatively dressed in a navy suit and white silk blouse. When she opened her mouth, I realized she was a cross between Madonna and Elly May Clampett. She double-checked with the upstairs "parlor" to see if I was expected. My appointment confirmed, she sent me up the stairway.

The upstairs area was furnished much like the downstairs, only the secretary's desk sat in front of a large set of cherry doors. The upstairs secretary was a carbon copy of the young woman downstairs. I was tempted to walk over to the railing and see if they did it with mirrors.

The blonde smiled at me. She must have had to explain frequently, because before I could say anything, she said, "We're twins. She's Tina and I'm Tammy."

I nodded at her and sat to look at various magazines and brochures in the sitting area. The magazines were all publications of CHOOSE GOD. Each of them was sprinkled throughout with appeals to the pocketbooks of all believers, the sad part being that those least able to afford it gave to these people. They in turn used it to build ostentatious structures under the pretense of glorifying God. If Jesus returns any time soon, he's going to own an awful lot of real estate.

Before I could become completely enraged at this sham of spirituality, Mordecai Bethune emerged from his office. He looked like Ronald Reagan, with a hint of used car salesman around the edges. His step was quick and he looked me in the eye, but his eyes made me uncomfortable. They had the sparkle of an extrovert, but seemed to close off any further knowledge of him. They were like blue steel doors that abruptly shut before you got through them.

"Mrs. Upchurch, praise the Lord, what a glorious day to be alive."

As he opened the door for me, I realized the carving on the cherry doors was of the Last Supper. We went into an office that could only be described as lush. In one of the matching wing chairs sat a man who was introduced to me as James Creech. James was a small, wiry man whose eyes moved quickly back and forth, even when he was speaking to you. This was in contrast to his body, which moved very slowly.

I looked at him again. This man? This was a man who inspired thousands on Sunday? Then, when James Creech opened his mouth, his voice was incredible to hear. Mesmerizing and invigorating at the same time, the kind of voice you would like to have when assigning your children Saturday chores.

The three wing chairs formed a triangle of sorts, and Mordecai indicated with his hand for me to sit in the one facing the door.

"James and I are very concerned that you understand that, while it is unfortunate that Mr. Richards is dead—"

"Murdered," I interrupted.

"Well, yes, murdered. We have no knowledge of his murder or anything of relevance to add to the information that the authorities have. Therefore, it would serve no useful purpose for our names and the name of the CHOOSE GOD denomination to be associated with the Iron Body Health Club."

The whole time he spoke James Creech nodded in agreement like one of those dogs that people sometimes put in the back of their cars. Their heads bob all the way down the interstate.

"I appreciate the delicate position you are in. However, I have a sister in jail and a nephew pumped full of steroids. I really don't have time for image preservation."

I had fibbed again; I did not appreciate the position they were in. If I didn't have other things to deal with I would have already turned this information over to Purdy to expose the whole thing.

Mordecai gave me a look which I assumed he thought showed great compassion. It was more like the "before" picture in an antacid commercial.

"We would gladly help your sister if we could, but that's not possible. We pray every day for the truth to be revealed."

"Did you know that Manly Richards ran an illegal steroid operation out of the Iron Body?"

Mordecai bowed his head and James followed suit. They shook their heads in unison.

"Mrs. Upchurch, we had no idea. Of course, your nephew is in our prayers."

There was that voice again.

"Why were you investing in the Iron Body Health Club?"

"Why indeed. We have many investments that we make, like any other individuals looking towards retirement one day. James and I also have stocks and bonds. We are but stewards of the CHOOSE GOD money."

"Was the investment profitable?"

There was a pause, very slight, but a pause nonetheless, that indicated Mordecai and James were thinking on this one. Mordecai laced the fingers of his hands together as if he was going to do the childhood rhyme, "Here is the church and here is the steeple, open the doors and see all the people."

"The venture had originally been profitable, but recently it was growing less and less so." He clinched his hands together, killing all the people in his church.

"What would you say if I told you that Manly's widow swears she heard Manly have a loud argument with you on the phone the week he died?"

"We did try and counsel Manly about some of the financial issues, but I can assure you, our end of that conversation was not heated."

A few more questions and answers made it obvious I was not going to get anywhere with these two men. I would have to turn my information over to J.C. and see if he could get any further. Of course, first I'd have to convince him to try. I was making progress in his willingness to pursue the case. The steroids must have upset him.

"Mrs. Upchurch, we need to make sure that all your questions have been answered. Neither James nor myself will be available for the next several days."

I stood. "I can't think of any others right now." I was careful not to promise that I wouldn't let anyone else in on our little secret. As I turned to get my purse, I got my first good look at the built-in bookshelves behind me. There were pictures of Mordecai Bethune with various conservative religious and political figures shaking hands and smiling. I had my picture made with a cardboard cutout of Elvis once, that's the closest I've come to fame.

I looked twice to make sure I was right. Down at the very end of the bottom bookshelf sat three videos exactly like the ones in the picture I saw in J.C.'s office. In the picture of the murder scene, there were three tapes on Manly's desk. The letters *VHT* were marked in red on their sides. The videos in front of me were the same brand with the same markings.

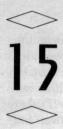

15

I opened my mouth to speak, thought better of it, and closed it. If these two were not going to be straight with me on other issues, they sure weren't going to tell me about those tapes. In fact, I was pretty sure that if I asked about them I'd probably never see those tapes again. I had to figure out some other way of getting them. I needed somebody to help me with that. I couldn't risk it on my own without a plan.

By the time I left the CHOOSE GOD compound, it was early afternoon. I circled back by Vicki's office for a quick chat. Martin was doing well, but events were weighing heavily on Vicki.

"Did I tell you about"—Vicki stopped in mid-question. She began to rummage through her purse.

I waited.

"Tell me about what?"

She pulled a tube of lipstick from her purse. "I'm sorry, what was I saying?" She began smearing her lips with an awful shade of orange. Her lips took on the appearance of pumpkin segments turned sideways.

Vicki and I were raised with the same rules. Applying your lipstick in public is up there with original sin. It was a true indication of the offender's proximity to trash. Being trash is the worst you can be; trash has never been strictly defined, but you know it when you see it. In Mama's ranking being trash is worse than being common.

"You were asking me if I'd heard about something."

She replaced the cover on the lipstick tube. "I wonder what."

"I really couldn't say." I tried not to sound irritated.

"Well, I did want to say I'm sorry for being rude at the hospital. It seems like there is so much going on and I can't seem to keep up."

"It's fine, I understand. You've got lipstick on your teeth." I pointed out the spot on my own teeth.

"Do I?" Vicki pulled a tissue from her purse and rubbed it across her teeth. "Joe Dan was saying last night . . ." Her hand was back in her pocketbook. She pulled the tube of lipstick out again and started all over, smearing it across her lips.

My fingers were itching to grab the tube from her. "What did Joe Dan say?"

"When?"

Vicki was not a good candidate to help get the tapes from CHOOSE GOD. I left her cleaning lipstick off her teeth for the second time and called J.C.

Since it was not a regular visitation day, he would have to make special arrangements for me to see Angel. I endured a few snorts and grumps. In the end,

I was limited to five minutes, but that would be plenty. Angel looked better than she had on Thanksgiving.

"Gee, Barbara, I missed you yesterday."

"I hate I couldn't make it over for visitation, but I thought you would have plenty of company with Mama, Daddy, Aunt Louise, and Uncle Harvey."

"I suppose so, and they brought me some more books to read." I could not figure out this newfound literary interest of Angel's. "You'll never believe who came to see me right before time was up?" She giggled into her plastic receiver.

"I can't guess, and we only have a few minutes."

"Madame Zsa Zsa. Isn't that wonderful?"

"I'm ecstatic. How did she get in here, anyway? She's not family."

"She's clergy, Barbara. Besides, she told me everything was going to be just great."

Clergy—that made as much sense as any of the rest of this. I doodled with my pen on my reporter's notepad. "Did she happen to tell you what she was doing at Manly Richards's house? I don't think the woman is on the up and up, Angel."

"Barbara, she has such honest eyes. I know she's right; everything is going to be okay. Did she tell you I'm going to get married soon?"

I started drawing jagged lines like lightning bolts across the page. "As a matter of fact she did, but I'm a little too preoccupied to start planning your trousseau. No doubt that will take a lot more effort than a groom."

Angel blushed. "I know you'll figure something out, Barbara." Four days ago, I was Miss Know-it-All. Today I was Jessica Fletcher. There in a nutshell was the problem with being a Type A person. Everyone knows you'll fix it. Never mind that you haven't got a clue, that your feet hurt, that you're starting to get varicose veins. A rock, me and the Prudential.

"Angel, have you got any idea what the tapes on Manly's desk were for?"

"What kind of tapes?"

"Videos, just regular videocassettes like you'd record on at home except they were marked with large red letters, *VHT.*"

"'Fraid not; do you think they're important?"

"Well, there were some on Manly's desk the night he was murdered. I need to find out what was on them because I've seen them somewhere else. I was thinking maybe you knew what Manly recorded on them."

Her blonde hair was French braided, and the bottom swung back and forth as she shook her head no. If you were going to call Angel a jailbird, it would have to be something showy, maybe a cockatoo. When our time was up, the jailer who opened the door for her was all smiles.

I was coming out of Lillington when I experienced that moment of aha. Right in the middle of the Cape Fear bridge, I looked up at a billboard that read, INVEST IN EDUCATION, with a big red apple and a yellow-bordered slate around it. Parents + Teachers = Success was written in white across the slate. Damn, in my excitement over the tapes, I had forgotten the conference with Miss Hudson about Melissa. I looked at the clock on the dash—three-ten. With a little luck and a lot of speed, I could make the elementary school by three-thirty.

Normally, I would have already called Edgar and

reminded him. But he needed to be weaned from the idea that I was in charge of remembering every birthday, anniversary, and other important dates and times for both our families and the free world. I figured I might as well start with something small like a teacher conference. I silently figured the odds that he would be there as I pulled into the emptying parking lot. To my surprise, his Wagoneer was parked at the edge of the lot.

When I went through the door into the classroom there Edgar sat, his knees pulled up unnaturally high because of the height of the chair. I made a mental note to give him a hard time about his ability to remember a school conference being directly related to how pretty the teacher was for the year. Miss Hudson was a brunette dynamo, a few years younger than Misty Jane. She had only been teaching two years and carried her enthusiasm for life into the classroom. Her hair was cut blunt to her shoulders, and she pushed it back over the top of her head with nervous energy as she talked.

It seemed that the note Melissa was passing the other day with Christy and Julie did have some of the test answers on it. In my mind I saw a newspaper with Melissa's picture on it. The headlines read "Tax Fraud" or "Embezzlement" across the top. I was bad at this sort of thing.

In the balance that nature provides married couples, Edgar has the ability to be even-tempered about these issues. He handled the discussion until I was able to make a rational comment. We assured Miss Hudson that we would have a talk with Melissa to see if we could figure out what was going on and to make sure it didn't happen again.

We gathered our jackets to leave. Miss Hudson glanced cautiously around and then, in a conspiratorial tone, said, "I understand Misty Jane has been having coffee with Joshua Merriwether."

I smiled. "It's true. She seems to have caught his eye." I tried to look nonchalant, like Misty Jane went out nightly with a different handsome doctor.

Miss Hudson lowered her voice. "Make sure she takes it slow. One of my college suite mates married his apartment mate from med school. She says he has several intendeds back at Duke."

"Several—"

"That's what she says. He nearly flunked out of med school keeping them all straight. Every one of them comes from money, too." Her tone conveyed her irritation. "Some guys don't know when they're ahead."

Miss Hudson seemed unnaturally concerned. I wondered if she was a love interest that hadn't worked out. "Did you ever connect with him? I'm mean, since you have a mutual acquaintance and all."

"Oh, we went out for coffee once, but that's all. I had the inside scoop on him." She shifted her weight and started stacking papers on her desk. Almost to herself, she said, "He really can be handsome and charming."

Partway through our exchange Edgar had gone out the door, waving his hand in our direction. He needed to get back to work, plus, not being a news reporter, he doesn't value these exchanges of everyday information that may come in handy someday. He calls them gossip.

I was on autopilot through dinner that night, nodding in time with Edgar when he sang Melissa the "You'd Better Stop Passing Those Notes and Cheating in Class Blues." We had agreed she would be grounded for a month. Discipline for parents as well as child.

Later, I lay on top of her rosebud comforter on the bed beside her. Her voice floated in the dark room. She admitted that she knew the answers but let Julie and Christy talk her into cheating because they thought it would be fun. We talked a little about letting other people make your decisions and how the consequences got bigger and bigger if you weren't able to say no.

"You can always tell your friends that you have the meanest mom in the world and she would kill you if you went along with them. I don't mind being an excuse to say no."

Melissa giggled.

I was restless in bed, trying to clear enough space in my mind to form a plan, which is hard to do when you keep rehashing the grocery list. A mother of three ought to be able to lease brain space from someone else now and then. When I pulled the covers off Edgar for the third time, he spoke up. "Slotp psulseoukng culrofvl."

He was lying on his stomach with his face in the pillow.

"I can't understand a word you're saying."

"I said give me back the covers and go to sleep. Honestly, Barbara, Melissa is going to be fine."

I parceled back some of the quilt to his side of the bed. "For your information, I've got other worries on my mind."

"Well, tell me about them so we can get some sleep. The *USA Today* version; I've got a busy day tomorrow."

Truthfully, I've never heard a man say, "Don't worry about it; we've got nothing going on at work tomorrow." Every day, the continued success of the business is dependent on them. Unless it is hunting season.

"Let me list them for you: Melissa, Angel, Martin, Mama, Vicki, and now, Misty Jane."

I told him what Miss Hudson had said.

"Maybe Miss Hudson is mistaken."

"Well, maybe she is and maybe she's not. I've still got to worry about it. I've got to figure out a way to get those tapes from Mordecai Bethune's office."

Edgar turned on his side. "Ask."

"I'm glad you thought of that." I popped him on the back with my pillow. "It certainly never occurred to me. The minute I ask for those tapes I can kiss them good-bye." I turned off the light again. "I need to think of a diversion."

"Count sheep," Edgar said and pulled a pillow over his head.

Communication is the key.

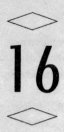

16

I called Alice at six-thirty on Tuesday. She gets up early to get Jameel off for his commute to State and Kecia out to Martinsboro High. I outlined the plan for her, and by the time I got to the office, she had taken care of getting Purdy's okay. I didn't ask her how much she'd had to tell him. A quick phone call confirmed the absence of Mordecai Bethune, while Alice explained the important issues of the day to Elaine from typesetting. Elaine covered for Alice when she was out.

Alice delighted in the thought of putting her dramatic talent to work. "From what you tell me, these two fluffs won't be hard to fool."

"I don't think so; why else would they idolize Mordecai and James? The offices and campus are lily white, so this will be sort of a reverse sociology field trip for Tammy and Tina."

"I've thought about going back to school when Kecia

graduates. Maybe this could be the start of my anthropological thesis, 'Monetary Religious Rituals in the Rural South.' I could be sort of a cross between Margaret Mead and Margaret Mitchell."

For her theatrical debut at CHOOSE GOD, Alice decided she would wear one of the flouncy dresses she'd worn in the early scenes of *Purlie*. The ruffles at the sleeves and the neck transformed her into a wide-eyed innocent. She dug a wide-brimmed matching hat with a ribbon out of a cardboard television box on the floor. She turned the flower and ribbon from the back to the front. It emphasized her deceptively young looks even more. I should be so lucky.

"Too much?" She put her palms flat on her face, imitating Macaulay Culkin in his now-famous mirror scene in *Home Alone*.

"I think even Tammy and Tina will have trouble buying that," I said.

She threw the hat back into the box. We walked back to the car.

This was going to be fun. If we pulled this off, we could do a program for the PTA, "Decoy Moves that Work." The program committee was constantly in search of new ideas.

"I don't know if I'll be able to keep a straight face when you get started. It's a good thing I'll be in the other room." I unlocked the doors and we got into the car.

Alice wrung her hands. "Lordy, Miss Scarlett, I don't know nothing about birthing no babies."

I turned the key in the ignition. "After all, tomorrow is another day. Know what I'm saying?"

⋄   ⋄   ⋄

Tina made sympathetic cooing noises when I explained about my lost reporter's pad and waved us on up the steps to Tammy. The twins were dressed in matching muted-peach sweater-and-skirt-sets—the form-fitting kind that I'm sure my form would have never tolerated even as an infant. Tammy greeted me with a smile that to her credit faded only slightly when I introduced Alice as my associate. I explained again about the notebook, wondering where my distortion of the truth put me in the stages of moral development. Tammy headed for the cherry doors.

"It won't take me a second to check for you."

I was right behind her. Our steps were muffled in the heavily padded carpet. I slipped through the door behind her when she opened it.

"I hate to bother you, especially when I can spot it faster than you."

She was looking back into the reception area and startled at the sound of my voice behind her. Tammy kept the door from closing by holding it with her hip. There was a yelp that I recognized as Alice's sudden attack of "kneeitis." Tammy gave an answering yelp and disappeared, the door, swinging soundlessly, closed.

I was at the shelf before the door swung shut, knowing I only had a few seconds at most to grab the tapes. I unzipped my black pocketbook as I moved. I searched the bottom shelf.

No tapes.

I looked over the top two shelves, thinking I'd remembered wrong.

No tapes. I had to have those tapes. I turned to the other bookshelf, reading titles as if I was in some fast-food library. VHT, VHT, where were they? I looked

wildly around the room, whirling to face the desk.
They had to be here somewhere.

I moved to the cherry credenza and heard Alice yell,
"Don't leave me!" our signal that I was running out of
time. Nothing on the credenza; I pulled at the drawers.
In the top one I glimpsed files and catalogs. Where could
the tapes be? I had a minute at most to find them. I
pulled open the bottom drawer, moving the hanging files
apart as I opened it. In the back, under the files, were the
tapes. Tammy would be there any second. I grabbed the
plastic cases. In one motion, I shut the drawer, took two
steps, and tucked the tapes in my bag. I zipped my bag as
I stepped towards the door. The door moved and I
bumped my knee against the desk in my haste to get
around it before Tammy had the door opened all the way.

Tammy's pale face appeared. "Your friend is hurt.
I—I don't know what's wrong."

I pushed past her and knelt down by Alice, who had
assumed a tragic pose on one of the couches, her ruf-
fled dress spread out around her.

"Alice, are you okay?"

She opened her eyes and winked at me from under
the safety of her hand. I nodded my head slightly so
she would know the tapes were ours.

"I think it's passed. It must have been my trick
knee."

My own knee was throbbing from its encounter
with the desk, and as I knelt I saw a large hole in my
pantyhose. I turned to Tammy and Tina, who had
arrived from her position downstairs to see what all
the commotion was about. Their eyes were showing a
tremendous amount of white around the royal blue of
their contacts.

"She could use some water."

They trotted off to the cooler in unison and returned with a five-ounce cup of CHOOSE GOD Plantation spring water in a paper cup with the CHOOSE GOD logo on it. I carefully placed my bag on the floor beside me, moving slowly so the black plastic video cases wouldn't clatter. Alice was sitting by this time, and I fanned her with a copy of the LTP magazine. Pat Buchanan was on the cover.

"Turn it the other way or I will be sick," Alice hissed at me.

I reassured Tammy and Tina. "I think she's fine. It'll help if she gets some fresh air on the way to the car."

"Did you find your notepad?"

"No, I sure didn't." I was able to look crestfallen thinking about the pair of pantyhose I had to replace.

Tammy smiled with a knowing air. "I told you it wasn't in there."

Alice and I made record time to the house. We had a celebratory Diet Mountain Dew and peanut bar in the car. The atmosphere in the station wagon reflected our giddiness. It felt like the first time you ever skipped school: You never do anything except drive around and feel self-satisfied that you aren't in class.

Alice put her feet up on the dash. "Those sweet girls are pitiful. I mean, I always wanted a large bust, but not if it was going to be bigger than my IQ."

"I imagine they have led a sheltered life. You were probably the most exotic creature they've come across."

"Don't you know it. Tammy and Tina, voluptuous bodies, no smarts—that's what I call TNT. I don't know if those girls would make it out here with the rest of us."

By the time we got to the house she was focusing less on their gullibility and more on her performance. In doing so she had determined she was Oscar material. I told her if anybody got an award it should be a Purple Heart for me on account of my knee.

I had no idea what the tapes were all about, but I prayed that they were something that would help Angel, hoping the divine spirit would let me slide on the way I got them.

The first tape came on. It took several minutes to figure out what was going on, considering the camera angle and everything.

Alice whistled low. "Girl, I'd say somebody is going to need an attorney. You think Arthur Talton was mad with you before, he is going to be really pissed now."

You know, people will surprise me occasionally; sometimes they'll amaze me, but these tapes horrified and saddened me at the same time. Except that they might help Angel. I couldn't figure all of what they would do for Angel, but at the very least I knew they would stir the pot so you could see all the stuff cooking down at the bottom.

"I'll bet you any amount of money that what you are looking at is the hot tub at the Iron Body Health Club."

"*Hot* is a key word; maybe *sick* is another." Alice turned away from the screen. "Do you think they know?"

"I bet not; I imagine these would be as big a surprise to them as they are to us."

The tapes contained images of women lounging in the hot tub at the spa and a lot more. Obviously, someone had rigged a camera so that they could enjoy a free show. Two of the biggest stars of the tape so far were

Tammy and Tina. Several other women who sported *National Geographic* breasts were not familiar to me, but I rarely met women in town in the buff. I had the tape on fast forward, and the images of breasts, appendages, and flesh whizzed across the screen. It was almost comic, but I felt no urge to laugh.

The tape continued and there was James Creech, in all his glory, with some women I didn't recognize. No wonder the reverends felt the need to give Manly money. Even though I wasn't responsible for the tapes, it still made me feel awful to watch them and to know that they would have to be seen by a lot more people before this was all over with. Alice must have read my mind.

"So what's the next step? J. C.? You gonna take these to him?"

"I am, just as soon as I check out the Iron Body and see if the camera location shows me anything. I think I may swing by and ask Tammy and Tina a few questions first. I hate to wait for the slow wheels of justice on this thing."

"That's fine with me, girl, but you know Purdy would kill for those tapes."

"I know."

She raised her eyebrows at me. "And, Barbara, if he'll kill for them, imagine what some other folks would do to you. Be careful."

Like a dutiful child, I promised Alice I would call her as soon as I arrived at J. C.'s office. I dropped her off at the newspaper office after I changed into some jeans and a sweatshirt. I looked in the full-length mirror on the back of the bathroom door. In one short clothing change I had become the unassuming house-wife; people take for granted that being home with children has dulled your wits. May as well use a stereotype to your advantage where you can.

Tammy and Tina were surprised to see me again, and very concerned about the state of Alice's health.

"She is fine, like she never even had a problem. I had a quick question for you. I was wondering if you two work out anywhere? You have such great figures."

To anyone else, my question might have been considered odd, but Tammy and Tina were not only not suspicious, they were flattered.

Tina blushed. "Actually, we work out all the time over at the Iron Body Health Club."

Tammy hastened to add, "The company pays for our membership so we feel like it would be wasteful not to go."

Tina's eyes opened a little wider and she leaned towards me. "We never see anyone else from here going. I guess they are not interested, but your body is a temple of God, you know."

"And exercise is a great way to relieve stress. I mean, we like working here and everything, but sometimes . . ." She gave me a look that was supposed to finish the sentence.

I returned the look. "Say no more. I know exactly what you mean. Thanks so much for the information. I'll keep it in mind."

I headed out the door and experienced only a moment of uneasiness when I passed Mordecai and James coming into the parking lot. They were supposed to be gone. As their black sedan disappeared from my rearview mirror, I let out a breath and pushed the gas pedal harder. I needed to get to the Iron Body Health Club as quickly as I could.

◦   ◦   ◦

The interior of the Iron Body was almost empty. The middle part of the afternoon was a slow time. Behind the desk was a young man with Brent Rogers, Front Desk Manager on his nametag. I had hardly met an employee of the Iron Body that didn't have a title; it must be one of those businesses that gives everybody a title so it doesn't have to pay them more money. I hadn't met Brent on my previous visits. He looked at me with the uninterested air of the self-absorbed young. Having been able to assess that I wasn't his type the minute I came in the door, he now concerned himself with folding towels.

"May I help you?"

I knew the area between the two locker rooms was occupied by the laundry equipment and pumps for the hot tubs. That was my guess as to where the camera might be.

"I certainly hope so. I've been trying to talk my husband into getting me a commercial dryer. We have five children and his mama and daddy living with us. And you would not believe the number of dryers we have been through. Do you have a commercial dryer?"

"Sure do, do you want to see it?"

"Would that be possible? I could use any information you have on it."

He came out from behind the counter. "I'll show you. Seeing as how I'm the front desk manager I know all about it."

I smiled encouragingly. "Really?" Good reporting is like being a therapist—the less you say the more you know.

"Man, you don't know mad until you have some lifter finish his workout and you have to tell him that he'll have to wait for a dry towel. These dudes can chew you up and spit you out."

The combination pump and laundry room was steamy and loud. We were surrounded by noise and movement. Two washers shimmied like they contained wild animals trying to get out, while beside them was a dryer with a digital readout above the round glass door. It was full of white towels being lifted and falling back to the bottom of the round cylinder only to be lifted again in one continuous motion. Behind the laundry equipment there were various boxes of detergents and shower soaps, cleaning supplies, and a large box of sweat-soaked clothing marked LOST AND FOUND with a red magic marker. There was a small closet that looked like a broom closet on the wall closest to the women's locker room. Beyond that, on both sides of the room were two concrete pits containing motorized pumps that were making a fairly loud hum, adding to the overall womb of noise.

Brent continued, "We have to buy tanks of propane to run the dryer. That's what those lines leading out the back are."

A shrill ring right above our heads startled me. Brent excused himself. I walked past the edge of the door when he was out of sight to hear him say, "Hey bro, how you doing?"

Great. Maybe he'd have a long conversation and forget about me. I moved quickly back to the wooden door of the broom closet. The doorknob refused to budge and the dead bolt above it was locked tight as well. I tried putting my eye to the crack by the doorjamb to see if I could see anything. No luck. J. C. was going to be the one who got to open this up. It was probably better that way, but I have to admit I was disappointed.

I walked back over to the door and stepped out of the noise to hear Brent say, "Later, dude." This I took to be the end of the conversation. By the time Brent returned I was examining the lint filter on the dryer.

"I really think this dryer would be too big for us."

We walked out to the front desk, where I feigned need of a rest room and proceeded into the women's locker room. The hot tub was in the back left corner. I pulled off my shoes and socks and stepped onto the ledge of blue tile that circled the hot tub. The steam rose, misting my skin and my clothes, making me feel like I was in a nervous sweat. Actually, I was in a nervous sweat, trying to keep my feet from sliding off the four-inch ledge. I felt comfortable negotiating with people; I was not that okay about tile ledges above bubbling 104-degree water.

There were silk ferns in brass pots on each corner, where the ledge widened. On both walls of the hot tub there were shelves with brass-potted silk plants that cascaded over the side of the shelf and down. Their green color gave a kind of mutant tropical feel to the steamy bath.

I went for the shelf on the farthest wall. Underneath the shelf, surrounded by plants, was a carefully concealed hole. Looking at it was enough to make me want to do in the reverends. Standing on that slick tile, I had the urge to go and find Tammy and Tina and give them a big hug. They were such babies anyway. It made my skin crawl thinking about it. These weren't just any men that were cinematically violating them. These lily-livered scumbags were people that they admired as men of God.

I started inching backwards and slipped. I teetered wildly, trying to regain my balance. My foot swung back and forth like the overtight pendulum of a clock and knocked a silk fern from its spot into the churning water. I regained my balance enough to plant my foot on the ledge and lean toward the wall for a minute, closing my eyes to calm myself. When I opened them, a movement at the edge of my vision caused me to turn. Brent was staring at me, his mouth compressed so that his lips were a small thin line. Did he think I was crazy or did he know about the camera?

"I'm a plant nut, too. My Harold is always telling me what a green thumb I am. I could have sworn those were real! Had to know for sure."

He blinked. Below me the fern was being rolled along by streams of water, coming up to the surface on top of a bubble and getting rolled down again. I still couldn't tell if he knew.

"Really, do you have any idea where they got those silk plants from? I'd love to have some to hang on the side porch. It doesn't get any sun."

"Look, lady, I don't know, but you've got to get down from there. You could hurt yourself and I'd be out of here for letting you do it."

"You think so?" I worked my way toward him. He held out a hand when I got within reach and I jumped down. I dried my feet with a towel he had brought in from the desk, slipped on my shoes and socks, and waved to him as I left. "Thanks for your help! I gotta run!" Judging from the look on his face, he thought I was a woman with a loose connection. He had his hand on the phone. No doubt to call in some reinforcements if I came back towards him.

I hurried toward the car, eager to get J.C. over there before anybody realized those tapes were missing. Mr. Otis McLamb was across the empty field checking something at the edge of the woods that define the perimeter of his property. I waved, rushed for the car, and hoped he wouldn't come over. I didn't have time for polite conversation. He turned back to his work and I breathed a sigh of relief.

It was a little premature.

Behind me a black BMW pulled into the parking lot. It had tinted windows and a squiggly car phone antenna sticking up from the roof in the center of the car's back window that made it appear like a demented space creature. Yuppie phone home.

The car door popped open and out stepped Mordecai Bethune. He did not look happy. I thought of the car trip with Alice and remembered that, after I'd skipped school that first time, I had engaged in a little conversation with the assistant principal and then spent some time in detention. That part came back to me now, facing an unsmiling Mordecai.

"I think you have something of mine."

"I don't think I do." I tried to sound casual, a posture I was having to imitate more and more lately. In fact, if I got much more nonchalant, you would be able to throw my arms and legs around like a Raggedy Anne doll.

"Mrs. Upchurch, I'm not in the mood to play games. The wrath of God is being revealed against all the godlessness and wickedness of men who suppress the truth by their wickedness. Give me my property. James."

Mordecai had developed a fine sweat across the top of his lip and sent every word across the space between us with force, trying to intimidate me as much as he could. James got out of the passenger side of the car and began to move with deliberate steps towards my car. Damn, where had I put the tapes? I knew the car was locked, but he would be able to see the tapes where I had stacked them in the car.

Too late, I wished Mr. Otis would be neighborly. Could I signal him? I turned to look for him, a dot at the far end of the field now. There was a hand on my wrist and, before I could move, Mordecai had pulled me within a couple of inches of his face. I pulled back as hard as I could, digging my sneakers into the black-top and screaming. I've had a recurring dream since I was in grade school that I would be in trouble and not be able to scream, so I put extra effort into it, slinging my handbag at James, who was coming up behind me. Mordecai released my hand and stepped back, sending me stumbling to keep from landing on my behind.

My thoughts of one-upmanship were short-lived. The reason for my sudden freedom had nothing to do with me. Buck Faircloth had pulled up in his red pickup truck. I wiped imaginary slime off my coat as I walked over towards his truck. He hopped out like an eager pup before I could get there. His arms and legs seemed to go everywhere at once. Unaware of what had transpired before he came into view, he nodded to the reverends.

"Barbara, I'm glad I caught you. Alice called from the newspaper all worried that something might have happened to you. It's a slow day, so I told her it was no problem, I'd handle it."

It felt like an escape from the class bully because the teacher had arrived. "Buck, that was mighty sweet of you. As a matter of fact, I was getting ready to head on back to the office, but thanks for checking on me."

He grinned. "If you wanted to you could put a good word in for me with Miss Angel."

"Sure thing." I wondered how it was men still referred to Angel as Miss Angel, like she was Miss Kitty on "Gunsmoke" or something. I waved at the reverends, who were now standing with the car doors open. "Buck, I need to check something with J.C. Will you hang around and keep your eye on things? It's possible someone would try to remove something from the crime scene. Nothing goes out of here until you hear from J.C., you understand?" I kept my arms close to my sides so no one could see I was shaking.

"Soon, Mrs. Upchurch, we will be talking with you soon," Mordecai Bethune said to me. Never would be too soon for me.

Buck turned to him. "Well, Reverend Bethune, you might want to make an appointment. Mrs. Upchurch, she's mighty busy these days."

I pulled out of the parking lot towards town. I couldn't get to the station fast enough. I squeezed my eyes to keep back the tears. I was two miles down the road before I could steady my hands long enough to unwrap a peanut bar. I didn't have time for a good cry.

17

Through the sliding windows by the dispatcher's desk, I saw Jackie reading. She must have heard me. Her chair squeaked and something thumped on the desk. I rounded the corner to see her straightening a pile of papers. Her brown hair was pulled back in a banana clip and shot from her head in all directions like Pepsi spraying out of a can. Before I was all the way through the door, she was talking.

"Barbara, would you please call Alice? She's 'bout worried the fool out of me. Calling every ten minutes. I was glad when Buck said he'd go check on you. And you're fine. That woman needs some pills for her nerves."

I wasn't really necessary to Jackie's conversation up to this point.

"Do you know where Buck got to? I promised J.C. we'd clean out the equipment closet, but I'm not about to start . . ." Her voice trailed off when she saw me.

"I need to see J. C." I'd managed to keep my voice steady, but my expression seemed to stop her one-way conversation. She took on the role of comforting friend. Motivated, I'm sure, in part by her natural disposition and in part by her curiosity.

"Hon, J. C.'s gone to Raleigh. I'm expecting him back any minute. You want me to give him a message or have him call you?"

I told her I'd wait. The phone rang and Jackie picked it up. Somebody's cat was in a tree. I held a palm to one ear and pointed with my other hand to indicate that I was going into J. C.'s office to use the telephone. She nodded in agreement and went back to making suggestions like, "Put a bowl of milk under the tree."

Conscious of my shoulder bag full of tapes, I pushed J. C.'s door until it was almost closed. In case Mordecai and James were bold enough to come looking for the tapes, I decided to put them under the desk. Alice picked up the phone on the second ring. She sounded relieved to hear from me, and I thanked her for sending Buck my way.

Alice lowered her voice. "Purdy has been after me to know everything. I've told him enough to let him know it's big stuff, but I left out all the uninteresting parts about you and me. Big picture stuff, you know?"

"Absolutely. No need to bore him with minor details."

"Speaking of minor details, Mitchell is on his way over. He should be there any time."

With the toe of my tennis shoe, I pushed the edge of my bag farther under J. C.'s desk.

"Great. I'm waiting for J. C. to get back from Raleigh. I'd like to be at the Iron Body when they find that camera."

"Call me if you need me, girl. Keep it together and don't let any more of the brethren lay hands on you."

"Not if I can help it." I hung up.

Next I called Edgar. "I've only got a minute. I'm in J.C.'s office."

"He arrest you?" Edgar laughed.

"No, he did not arrest me. For your information, today I have uncovered pornographic videos, been physically threatened by a man of the cloth, and found out about the most candid camera going. All before suppertime."

"Why is it that when I'm with you we do things like go to the Hanging Dog Christmas parade, but the minute my back is turned you're out finding porno?"

"You're not living right, I guess."

"I assume this porno is what you and Alice went after this morning."

"It is, and I think the reverends are about to do a Humpty Dumpty right off their wall. Maybe into jail."

"The reverends liking risqué movies is not going to make them very popular with their followers, but it certainly isn't illegal."

"There is a little more to it than that. Like people being filmed when they had no idea they were on camera. I can't go into it all right now, but the reverends' home movies are more than risqué. They are quite adamant about wanting them back." I filled him in on my parking lot experience.

"When J.C. gets there you're going to give him the tapes and leave." It was half-statement, half-question.

"I'm only staying until I'm sure they aren't going to delay going to look for the tapes until it's too late."

"Barbara, I'm serious now. Don't you think it's time for you to come on home and let J.C. handle this?"

"Edgar, I can't quit now. Picture this. You're at the mill. Corporate suits everywhere. Time for you to make a big presentation. I call and insist you come home; your workload is too heavy and we need to see you. We both know the suits would win."

"For one thing, you'd never do that—"

"Exactly."

"Don't interrupt. For another thing, the suits aren't going to shoot me if I make a bad presentation. Barbara, I'm worried about you. If anything happens to you, I'll be cooking dinner the rest of my life."

I didn't have time to stand and fight with Edgar. I had to get him back to being practical. "Supper, now there's a magic word. I need you to pick up the kids, too, please."

Edgar sighed loudly. "I suppose I can get that fried chicken from Hardee's."

"You could cook."

"Chicken is looking better all the time. I think this is five nights in the last week. I'm going to start keeping count."

"Good, because by my calculations you have roughly ten thousand more meals to go before you catch up with me."

"I'm the engineer; don't try to talk numbers with me. It does me no good to say this, but don't drive home by yourself. Get J.C. to follow you, or I'll come up and drive back with you. Misty Jane can stay with the kids."

"Okay."

"I mean it, Barbara. It is not okay to go off by yourself

until J. C. gets these men under control. I'm going to call J. C. if that's what it takes."

I was annoyed. "I said okay." Like calling J. C. was going to make me do something. Edgar knew better.

"Would it make you happy if I said go ahead get yourself killed? You get mad because I don't pay attention to things and now you get mad because I do."

"I wish you'd pay attention to anniversaries and when the laundry needs to be done. But this is no time to argue. I love you." The last statement was said in the most exasperated tone I could manage.

J. C. came in as I was hanging up the phone. "Jackie spoke to Buck a minute ago. This had better be good. Newspaper business must be slow for you to keep after my people all the time."

"There is good reason. It's right here in my pocketbook." I pulled my bag from under his desk. I went through my day, not explaining how I got the tapes, but telling him what they contained and about checking the Iron Body hot tub and the parking lot meeting. By the time I'd finished, J. C. was out at Jackie's desk with the tapes in his hand.

"Get Buck on the phone. Tell him nothing leaves the Iron Body until I get there. Find Ed and tell him I need him to go over to the CHOOSE GOD compound and radio in when he gets there. I'm going to the library. Barbara, stay here until I get back."

In the back room of the library was a VCR that was used for children's story hour. I must admit, J. C. moved faster than I'd seen in a while. His legs shuffled along at a pace somewhere between the two-step and a trot.

Jackie signed off the radio with Ed. "Been a while

since I've seen J.C. move that fast. Tapes must be pretty interesting."

"To the right people, I would think so."

"You've lost weight, haven't you, Barbara? I can see it in your face." Jackie was stretching hard to find out what was in those tapes.

"Must be that I got my hair trimmed."

"Guess you're relieved those tapes prove Angel's innocence?"

"I'm not at all certain what those tapes prove, Jackie. That's why I'm letting the law enforcement professionals handle it."

Jackie picked up her copy of *Soap Opera Digest*. She held it at the right angle to read and glare at me at the same time. When she heard J.C. coming back down the hall, she tossed it onto the desk.

Between the door and his office he'd told her to call Pete in for backup at the Iron Body and to call Raleigh and see if Agent Bailey was available. He locked the tapes in a cabinet and then locked his office.

Mitchell had come in the door right after J.C.

"Chief Spivey, any word we have a breakthrough in the Iron Body murder?" J.C. grunted. "Anything you can tell us about possible illegal activities at the Iron Body?" J.C. stepped in Mitchell's direction. Mitchell quickly stepped back, knocking over the metal trashcan. J.C. grabbed a handheld radio from the top of the file cabinet. Deciding he was safe, Mitchell brushed himself off and continued.

"Are you prepared to make a statement?"

"No."

"Is this tied to the steroid investigation?"

"No." J.C. never looked at him, swatting at his

questions with one-word answers like they were flies. Mitchell stationed himself behind Jackie.

"Chief Spivey, does the public need to be concerned for their safety?"

J.C. stopped. "Son, if you'll quit asking so many damn foolish questions and open your eyes you might learn something."

Mitchell followed us out to the parking lot. "Where are we going now? To the Iron Body?" J.C. ignored him. I opened the car door and threw my pocketbook onto the seat.

"Yes, Mitchell. Did you bring the camera?"

"Barbara, I am a professional." He slammed the door of his Camry.

Agent Bailey arrived at the Iron Body minutes after we did. "I was in the area already," was all he said. He avoided looking directly at J.C. or myself, which is a worrisome sign in man, child, or beast. I couldn't figure what was going on with him. I harbored pictures of him as a sinister criminal using the SBI resources for crimes involving drugs and videos of naked women. How much did SBI agents make anyway?

He must have had similar thoughts about me, because he asked J.C. what I was doing there. I could not hear J.C.'s muttered reply, but it seemed to appease Agent Bailey. J.C. reminded me of a cross between a pit bull and a bloodhound. He had the scent of something and he wasn't letting go until he treed it or ripped it to shreds.

Manly's office, the murder scene a few days earlier, now experienced a bustle of activity. J.C., Agent

Bailey, and Pete went off to the room that housed the dryer. Buck stood guard at Manly's door. After Pete went to the truck twice for tools, J.C. and Agent Bailey reappeared and moved back to Manly's office, leaving Pete to guard the laundry room door until the lab staff arrived. Patrons in spandex and warm-ups veered in a large circle around the door to Manly's office.

Buck smiled at them. "It'd help us out a whole lot if y'all could stay on the other side of that desk," he politely requested of each.

Brent Rodgers was behind the front desk in conversation with Peter York. Brent called Peter shortly after the army of law enforcement types descended upon the Iron Body. Peter arrived and blustered a bit about search warrants, but J.C. walked away from him without so much as a "Sorry for your inconvenience."

J.C. bumped into a guy wearing blue workout shorts and a Martinsboro High T-shirt as he was coming out of the laundry room. "That does it." He was at the counter leaning over into Peter York's face. "This ain't the picture show. Get these people out of here."

"Yeah, well, all right, but I'm going to have to answer to those guys up in Raleigh and they are not going to be happy." Peter's lip curled slightly.

Unhappy was an understatement at this point. J.C. moved on back towards Manly's office. "Give them my phone number."

Peter watched J.C. go into Manly's office. Then he walked from behind the front desk counter, snatching open the hinged access and slamming it back down. He moved in circles around the exercise crowd, herding them up and moving them toward the locker room, backtracking every now and then to get a stray.

Mitchell and I were standing at the door to the office. I stood on my toes and tried to look over Buck's shoulder. J.C. stepped back out. He pointed to a gray carpet-covered bench. "There, right there. You two don't stay right there, you're outside. Understand?"

Mitchell held up his pad. "You will make an official statement, won't you?"

J.C. walked back into the office and closed the door. I made conversation with Buck, who had stationed himself across the door in a Matt Dillon stance. Mitchell got up, snapping pictures.

"Barbara, you're in the picture. Move to the right."

I folded my arms across my chest. "Your mother ever teach you the magic word?"

"Oh, for God's sake, please."

I moved to the end of the bench.

Mitchell snapped the picture. "I don't have to tell you, Buck, that picture could end up on the front page. Can you tell me anything about the crime?"

"Nope."

"Any suspects?"

"Nope."

"What can you tell me?"

"Chief told me to stand right here and not let anybody in unless he said so."

"Well, that's certainly front-page stuff."

Peter York walked over to Buck. "Jackie's on the phone for you."

Buck pointed his finger at his chest. "Me?"

"Your name is Buck, right? Well, the police chief said to give you the call; he's in the middle of something."

Buck looked at him. "Chief told me to stay here."

I got up and moved toward the front counter. "I'll see what she wants, Buck."

Mitchell got up to follow. "Purdy is not going to like it one bit if you don't help me get this story."

"Who said I wasn't going to help?"

Jackie didn't want to give her message to me.

"Say it in code or something. Everybody is busy over here." I was becoming impatient. On the counter the towels left by the retreating patrons smelled musky and damp, gym sock stuff.

"Look, tell J.C. to get on the phone. Ed wants to know what to do next and he doesn't want to talk about it on the radio."

"Hold on; I'll see what I can do."

I walked back over to Buck. "Listen, Jackie says Ed is on the phone. He needs to talk to J.C., but he doesn't want to talk over the radio."

Buck twitched his eyebrows at me. Then he turned and opened the door a crack. "Chief, Ed is on the phone. Can't talk over the radio because of his 10-20."

Papers rattled. J.C.'s voice came through the open doorway. "Damnation. Do you have to punch the button on this phone or what?"

Peter York yelled, "Whoa man, wait a minute! I've got to put it on hold before you can pick up!"

J.C.'s voice again. "You're at Arthur Talton's? Good. I'm getting ready to call over there and invite everybody to the station for a party. You follow them and make sure they get there."

Ed had found the reverends. The phone banged down. "Buck, shut the door."

Buck grinned at me. "Jackie must really be having

fun. I thought for sure she was calling to tell me her shift was up. It's my night to relieve her." It's the little things in life that make you happy.

I phoned Sam Quakenbush and caught him as he was leaving the office for the day. When I explained the situation to him, he assured me he would go on over to J.C.'s office and hang out during the questioning. He promised to let me know if there was any news that would help Angel.

I decided to go home while the going was good. Without a doubt, J.C. wouldn't let me anywhere near the reverends, and, in their present state of mind, Edgar was right, I didn't want them anywhere near me. I called to let Edgar know I was on my way. It was almost six-fifteen and completely dark out.

"Somebody going to follow you home?"

I rubbed my neck. "Everyone here is busy."

"I'm coming to get you then."

"All right, all right. I'll see if J.C. can spare Buck. If not I'll get right back to you." I was too tired to argue.

The smell of Hardee's fried chicken greeted me at the door. It was followed by Edgar and the three children. There were hugs from Edgar and the youngest two. I didn't get a hug from Becky, but she was eyeing me with new respect.

"Did you really get Aunt Angel off the hook?"

I shot Edgar a look.

"No details; I told them you'd found some new suspects."

"Totally awesome, Mom." Jason jumped onto the couch and clicked on the TV. How fleeting fame is, especially with your children.

"We don't know if she's home free yet."

Edgar threw his arms around Melissa and me and started towards the kitchen. "We saved you a chicken breast. I've had to threaten the kids within an inch of their lives if they touched it."

The phone rang, which was like the bell of the starting gate for the kids, everyone running for glory. Becky started talking upstairs and everyone else went back to other things, vowing to win next time. Edgar sent Melissa to the refrigerator to get me a Diet Mountain Dew.

"Everyone has been calling—Purdy, Alice, your mom, my mom, Vicki, Ladawn—"

"Mom! Telephone," Becky screamed from the top of the stairs. That was the last bit of peace and quiet for the rest of the night.

18

The call was from Purdy, who had pounced on the idea that I was personally responsible for how slow the wheels of justice turn. He was not going to let it go, since he was holding up the paper for the story. Also, he'd gotten a call from Arthur Talton threatening to sue if any slanderous statements were made against his clients, or if any tapes illegally obtained were used by the media. I assured Purdy I had no tapes or new information. He would have to go to press with what Mitchell could get.

I decided not to worry about Arthur Talton; his two clients were in such hot water it would be a while before they could come after me. I made a mental note to ask Sam Quakenbush about what might happen to someone who picked up tapes in an office that didn't actually belong to them.

Between telephone conversations, the children told me the news of their day. I reminded each of them they needed to locate all their winter paraphernalia in case it should turn cold. They were all riding on floats in Saturday's parade. Edgar made the last call for bed, and toilets flushed as they settled for the night.

Sam stopped by at about ten o'clock. Edgar answered the door and I said a prayer of thanks that he'd made the children pick up the family room after supper.

Edgar reached for Sam's hand. "A lawyer making house calls; I don't know if we can afford this."

Sam looked around. "You got a second mortgage on this house, yet?"

They laughed. Sam turned to me. "Sorry to be so late, Barbara, but these things take time. It was worth it tonight."

"You have good news?"

"Angel will be released in the morning."

I laughed and cried, letting out all the emotions of the past week at one time. I hugged Edgar. I hugged Sam. I hugged Edgar again. I don't think I realized until that moment how uptight I had been about Angel's arrest.

I remembered my manners and offered Sam some coffee. He refused, but sat on the couch to give us details.

"It seems that Mordecai Bethune and James Creech were at the Iron Body on the night of the murder. Mordecai says they went by to talk with Manly about some management issues. Both of them categorically deny any knowledge of the tapes and say they had nothing to do with the three left on Manly's desk. Even when J.C. prodded them by saying that it wouldn't take long to match the set of fingerprints on the tapes with theirs, they still repudiated any knowledge of them. Mordecai said the tapes were made without his knowledge or consent, and moving about Manly's office he might have touched them, so naturally they would have his prints."

"Does J. C. believe him?"

"I don't think so. But in my opinion, he may have trouble proving otherwise."

Never ask a lawyer an open-ended question. After Sam had talked on a few more paragraphs, I gave him a verbal nudge. "This doesn't affect Angel, though, does it?"

"Not directly. What is significant for Angel is that Mordecai and James swear that they drove into the parking lot at the Iron Body at ten-twelve P.M. by the clock in Mordecai's car. They had a ten-fifteen appointment with Manly and never went before ten anyway, even though the club closed at six on Sundays. They were not interested in meeting any of the club's patrons. Sunday they couldn't go any earlier because they were tied up at church until after nine. Manly was dead when they walked into the office."

Angel didn't leave the truck stop before ten that night. She had several dozen witnesses to that, so it would have been impossible for her to have killed Manly. My body was having trouble handling the rush of adrenaline my brain was sending it. I found myself knotting and unknotting a necklace I had picked up off the coffee table, using my nervous energy.

"Why haven't they come forward on their own before now?" Anger tightened Edgar's voice. "There was a woman's life at stake."

"They swear they would have come forward at trial.

They had no idea that Angel had an alibi for earlier in the evening. They thought she'd done it."

"They had no idea they would get caught is more like it. They sat right in front of me Monday and swore they had nothing that would be of any use to Angel, miserable scumbags that they are. What keeps anybody from believing they didn't kill him themselves?" I didn't see how it could be any other way.

"Not much evidence at this point, though I'm sure J.C. and Agent Bailey will do everything in their power to find some. The other interesting thing is that Mordecai and James insist that Manly asked them to come after ten-fifteen that night because he had another appointment."

"Well, of course, they would say anything to clear themselves. I sure hope J.C. isn't going to fall for that. I'm willing to bet—"

Edgar interrupted me. "The main thing right now is Angel is out. We need to let Sam get home, and you can talk about this tomorrow when you know more."

I agreed, thanked Sam, and set up an eight o'clock appointment to meet him the next day at the jail.

I sat at the table and called the family to let everyone know that Angel would be a free woman in a few short hours. The conversations were emotional, and it was agreed that I would pick her up and get her over to Mama and Daddy's house as soon as possible. If she weren't up to staying back at her apartment, then she could stay with Mama and Daddy for a while. Mama wanted everyone to come on Friday evening for a retake of Thanksgiving, since the week before we hadn't been particularly festive or thankful. I agreed to make more pecan tarts and more broccoli casserole, reaching for a yellow sticky note to write myself a reminder.

I was alternately ecstatic and angry over the turn of events. It would be immoral if the reverends didn't have to pay for their crimes. I was not consoled by Mama's thought that they would pay for them in the hereafter. That was not soon enough for me. I reached into the refrigerator for some milk, hoping a glass would settle me down, noting as I did so our supply wouldn't last past breakfast in the morning. I really needed to get by the grocery store. The children, the house, the dog, and Edgar could all use some attention. We always put the Christmas tree up by the first weekend in December, which was this weekend. I felt tired thinking of it all. The shower was hot and released some of the tension in the muscles of my neck and shoulders. I got out and threw on an oversize cotton T-shirt and toweled the ends of my hair, which had gotten wet.

Edgar was reading when I crawled into the bed. We have a tall, pine four-poster. I reached over and kissed him good night, burrowing into the sheets to make a nest for sleep. My mind wouldn't shut off. I burrowed again, pulling my legs a little closer and propping my left arm with a pillow. My mind was still making grocery lists and trying to remember when Melissa and Jason had basketball practice on Saturday. Both played in the town recreation league. Interspersed with this was a judge leaning over the bench and declaring Mordecai and James guilty. Five minutes later, when I changed position the third time, Edgar reached over and rubbed my shoulder. "Too tense to sleep?"

"Uh-huh. Rub my neck, will you?"

His hand kneaded the muscle of my neck and they loosened under his warmth. His other hand reached under the hem of my T-shirt, brushing lightly across my thigh.

"I know something that will really relieve that tension."

I turned my head towards him and kissed him. "No doubt."

The brushing of my thigh became a little more spirited. I still had the grocery list running through my head.

"Works for me." He got up to secure the bedroom door against wayward children. I tried to remember if I had enough vanilla to make those tarts one more time.

He got back in bed and pulled me to him. I would need to check the spice cabinet. His hand traveled along my thigh leisurely. Dr. Ruth and Ann Landers both will tell you, good sex originates in the most vital organ, the brain. I moved closer to him and pushed the grocery list from my mind.

19

The next day, with the exception of getting Angel and delivering her to my parents' house, was uneventful. I did not complain. True to form, Angel looked like she had been on a Carnival cruise ship for the last week, not a guest of the county. I must admit I felt a tweak of jealousy when Mama and Daddy fell all over her as if she were a returning hero. What good did it do to be the Wise Virgin if nobody ever noticed you had oil in your lamp?

I made it to the grocery store, talked with Vicki on the phone, and confirmed with Ladawn that I would be at the parade committee meeting on Friday. Then I refused to answer my phone, screening my calls with the answering machine. I cleaned house.

Cleaning can be therapeutic. Some people play tennis, some people jog, I clean. I name every spot on my linoleum. It's my answer to testosterone. While others are out pushing and shouting to prove they're macho, I simply wipe people out with a brush of my mop. In my kitchen on that Wednesday, I got Mordecai, James, Arthur Talton, and many others. They were gone, leaving only the scent of Pine Sol behind them. By the time I picked the children up from school, I was feeling so much better that I went to Jazzercise that night.

My arrival at the office on Thursday received a mixed review. The day was headed for the sixties which is a little above normal for the Piedmont of North Carolina in December, so I wore a matching turtleneck and sweater in red and black with my jeans skirt. I went by the Dash Mart and picked up two coffees and two danish on my way to work. After all, I did go to Jazzercise the night before. Alice and I talked while we ate. She said Arthur Talton had been by and Purdy had held his ground with him.

"I don't know if I'd believe it if I hadn't seen it myself. Purdy pulled his little self up to his full height, which was about to Arthur's belly button, and told Arthur to get his big talk and his big bottom out of his office." She poured half-and-half into her coffee. "Made me want to kiss him, so you know I was impressed."

I invited her and her husband, Reginald, to our get-together that Friday. She promised she'd check with him to see if he had plans.

"Kecia and Jameel are welcome to come along as well."

She stirred her coffee. "Thanks for the invite, but you know those two have got better things to do than hang around with their parents."

"Well, at least they will admit to having parents. Becky is at the age where she likes people to think she came out of the earth fully formed. Then she doesn't have to acknowledge Edgar or myself."

I picked up my coffee and headed back towards my office. Jay seemed glad to see me. I thanked him again for helping me out on my stories. Even Mitchell was nice, since I'd done him a favor at the club on Tuesday night. I think he was actually a little in awe of me, being that someone might sue me and the paper over what I had done. That didn't mean that he wasn't staying as far away from the reverends' names in his stories as he could and still preserve our "journalistic integrity."

When Mitchell left the room to go across the street for a cup of coffee, Jay confided in me that Mitchell had tried his best to get Jay to take the story. Velena came in to do her column and ignored me. Obviously, she didn't take too kindly to me messing with men of God. Alice had mentioned earlier that on Wednesday afternoon she'd made some shrill comment about the saints being persecuted and handmaidens of the devil. I've been called worse. Velena was the kind of woman who would continue sending these men money even after they'd proved to be lower than low.

Alice buzzed my extension and told me that Purdy had arrived and wanted to see me.

He came around his desk and gave me a big hug when I walked in the door. I had on flats, so he was almost at eye level with me. He was dressed casually, knit shirt and loud plaid pants. We sat facing each other in the chairs in front of his desk.

"Going golfing today?"

"They say the weather's supposed to turn real cold by Saturday, so I thought I'd take the rest of the day and hit a few rounds with Judge Thomas."

He placed emphasis on his words so that I couldn't mistake that his choice of a golf partner was significant.

"Barbara, I've consulted with Robert Morse." Robert Morse is the *News Herald*'s attorney. "I'm not sure how clear-cut this thing with the video is going to be. These guys really have Arthur kicking up as much dust as he can. He's saying they'll go after you and Alice for stealing and unlawful entry and the paper will be named an accessory." He looked down at his desk, a sudden interest in his blotter. "The worst that will probably happen is that we'll run up a large bill with a lawyer. We'll have Robert working on it, but I didn't know if you might want to go ahead and consult an attorney."

I could feel the blush creeping up my face.

"The paper's backing you all the way, of course, and if you don't want to hire anyone else to help that's fine. I'll arrange for a conference with Robert."

I pushed up out of the leather chair. "Doesn't it seem a bit cockeyed to you that Alice and I discover that these two men are nothing more than slime, wolves in sheeps' clothing, exploiting innocent people and possibly murdering someone, and Alice and I are the ones with the problem, not them?"

"They are by no means free and clear, and Robert doesn't think they have a case."

"Oh, come on, Purdy, why should Alice and I have to defend ourselves in a court of law at all? Why?" I could feel my body tighten. This was incredible. I was concerned about what might happen to me, but more about what I might have gotten Alice involved in.

"I know it will all work out, Barbara, but I thought you ought to know what's going on and make some decisions before anything else happens."

"Does Alice know?"

"No, I thought you should know first."

I pressed my hands to my face. "Well, I'll talk to her, don't worry about it. Let me know if anything interesting happens on the golf course."

He nodded and I moved back into the reception area. Alice was at her desk. While I talked she stuffed trash from her desk into her Dash Mart Styrofoam coffee cup. Then she sailed it in a perfect arch to the trash can, where it landed with a thunk.

"Girl, I have got it in the bag. You go on about whatever it is you need to get done."

"Do you want to come see Sam Quakenbush with me? My treat. I'm sure he is going to start giving my family quantity discounts anyway."

She put her hand on my arm. "I haven't come from where I did to let a couple of white SOB perverts take me down. I'm telling you, trust me."

Our conversation was loud, and Purdy had come to his door, sending an unspoken message by glancing around casually and then walking back to his chair.

I lowered my voice. "Okay. I suppose I shouldn't ask?"

"You could, but I'll only tell you one thing. You were given the tapes."

"I was?"

"You were. Tammy gave them to you."

The phone rang and Alice answered it, waving me off. I went on back down the hall and called the middle school to confirm the band's Christmas concert on the twelfth. J. C. called about thirty minutes later and asked when I could come to the station. I told him I'd be there right after lunch. No later than one, he said. He had an midafternoon appointment with the mayor.

I was there by twelve-thirty, my curiosity getting the best of me. J.C. ushered me into his office, all business, and closed the door. He leaned against his desk and pointed to a chair in front of him for me. "You realize Mordecai Bethune and James Creech are after your tail end?"

"So I hear."

"You want to tell me where you got those tapes?"

I felt like one of the Israelites stepping onto the floor of the Red Sea; the water formed high walls around me, and I wasn't sure if they would come crashing in or not. Behind, the Egyptians were in hot pursuit. Some choice. "Tammy gave them to me."

J.C. scratched his neck and shifted his leg on the desk. "Have you talked to Tammy since then?"

"Only once, when I went back and asked if she and Tina were members of the Iron Body." So far, so good.

"Well, it's damn amazing to me. Those girls told me the same thing. Sat right across this desk from me yesterday evening, smiling and twisting their hair." He jerked his head in the direction of the desk behind him. "Said they thought you were supposed to have those tapes so they went in Mordecai's office and gave them to you. Tammy tells me this and Tina tells me she was an eyewitness to the whole thing. Alice is going to come down here after work. No doubt, she'll tell me the same thing."

"I imagine she will." I was so close to that Red Sea water I could smell the salt.

"The funny thing is I didn't show Tammy and Tina the tape until after I got their statements. I asked them to be real sure. I told them, It's going to get your boss in a hell of a lot of trouble. Excuse my language.

That Tammy twists a piece of her hair and says it brings tears to her eyes thinking about it."

I felt my foot hit dry land on the other side of the sea, and made myself a note to check on Tammy and Tina after this settled down. Maybe they could file a lawsuit, get a piece of the rock, or, in the case of CHOOSE GOD, the bricks.

"I don't know how you did it, but all I've got to say is congratulations. These men belong behind bars. It's possible we can arrange it. The mayor and the county commissioners are in a big hassle over this thing. Hell, the mayor's wife belongs to that club. They could've got her on video for all we know. The mayor wants something done now, and the county commissioners want to tell me how many jobs these two provide for the county. We're having a special meeting this afternoon. I sent Buck out to get me the biggest thing of Tums he could find." J. C. was rolling now, pounding his desk for emphasis. "This is an upsetting thing to a lot of folks, jobs or no jobs. The phone has rang all day. I tell you, smut is smut no matter who does it. I've heard of holy smoke, but I've never heard of holy smut." He grinned. "I'm going to have to remember that one for the county commissioners."

It was a good time to try for information. "Did you ever get back those computer checks on Madame Zsa Zsa and Bunny Richards?"

"And what if I did? I can't go telling you that kind of stuff. Their past records are their business."

"So they do have past records?"

"I didn't say that. We're looking at everybody as a suspect now that Angel is in the clear."

"Well, I hope the reverends are at the top of the list. Don't you have enough to get them for killing Manly?"

"We're pursuing some things, but we don't have any real evidence to tie them to the murder. And we're going to have to be real tricky on this video thing or we may lose it. Not to mention, we still are looking for the source of those steroids."

"Speaking of real tricky, how long have you known Agent Bailey?"

"Several years, why?"

"He seems sort of suspicious to me. You've never have figured out who killed Wiley, have you?"

"Damnation, Barbara Gail, you don't get yourself out of one mess before you're trying to get in another one. For your information, Agent Bailey is a fine man. Been through some rough times the last few years; his wife ran off and left him for another woman. No children, though—I guess it's just as well."

I realized the pain I was seeing on J.C.'s face was his and Eunice's over never having children of their own. What would happen if one left the other? Would their years together count if there wasn't the tangible evidence of children, instead of Lucy's ceramic statues? It made me feel a little selfish for all those times I'd wanted to go off to Tahiti.

"J.C., grief leads people to do strange things."

"Strange, Barbara Gail. I tell you, strange. You stand here much longer and I may send you off to Lillington to be locked up as a material witness. How'd you like them apples?" He stood and motioned toward the door. There was a black satchel on the desk behind him.

"Is that your bag?" I pointed. I had not forgotten Madame Zsa Zsa's little "vision."

"No, that belongs to the Reverend James Creech. He brought it over here stuffed full of church literature. Like that was going to have some bearing on the whole thing."

I still wasn't ready to think the reverends didn't have something to do with Manly's murder.

J. C. followed me out to the car and warned me that I ought to be careful. No matter if charges were filed against Mordecai and James, they would have bail in a matter of minutes and walk free until their trials. I got in, throwing my bag on top of the dry cleaning I needed to remember to take to the cleaners. Clean clothes stop for no man (or woman, for that matter). I shut the door and rolled down the window, enjoying the warm cocoon the sun had created inside.

J. C. leaned across the door. "If these guys are only a couple of perverts they will probably leave you alone, but if they're cold-blooded murderers that's a different story. Keep out of the way until we can figure out which they are."

20

I did my best over the next two days to stay out of the way. It happened to be one of the rare occasions when my best wasn't good enough. The paper came out late on Thursday and contained only brief details of the tape scandal and a quick blurb about Angel's release in which she thanked everyone for helping clear her of the charges. This time there was a nice picture of her with Mama and Daddy, looking as if she'd stepped from a glossy fashion ad instead of my station wagon.

Edgar worked late Thursday to catch up on all the stuff he had missed in the last week. I fixed the children peanut-butter-and-banana sandwiches and a fruit salad and hoped Mrs. Upchurch wouldn't come by before they were through.

After supper, Vicki called to tell me that Misty Jane was bringing Joshua Merriwether to the party at Mama's on Friday. I lectured myself the whole time on why I would not mention Miss Hudson's comments about him to Vicki. I liked Miss Hudson, but maybe her concern wasn't as genuine as it appeared. Besides, if Misty Jane brought him to dinner, I could get to know him up close and personal and form an opinion of my own.

Vicki also mentioned that the county manager and the commissioners were stomping and fuming when they came in from the meeting with J.C. and the mayor. I guess our team had held its ground. She was afraid the county manager might have an aneurysm. The tension was so bad *she* had to take two Tylenols and lie down for a few minutes on the ladies' room couch.

I got the children settled for bed, and Edgar called to say he was on his way home. Melissa was sniffling into her pillow, and I went to check on her, taking along a tissue from the bathroom. Christy and Julie had teased her because I worked and their mothers didn't. Her voice quivered through the darkness. "They said their mothers said we were poor."

I hate it when small-town people act small. I rested my head back on Snuggles, the bear. "That's not true, Melissa, I don't work for the money. If Christy and Julie's mothers knew what Purdy paid me they'd know that."

She sniffed into the tissue.

"We won't ever be rich, but we could get by on what your dad gets paid. I work for other reasons. It helps exercise my brain, and most of the time makes me feel good about myself when I see a story with my name beside it or when I know I asked the right question. It's that same feeling you get when you hit the ball in softball. You know the feeling I'm talking about?" I felt her move her head beside me. "Maybe you'd like to come to work with me one day and see what I do. The world contains so many possibilities and it's a real shame, in fact, between you and me, it's a sin, to shut yourself off from different people and things only because they're different, before you know enough about them to know if you like them or not." I don't know if my words made her feel any better, but they helped me.

"When can I go to work with you?"

"Soon." I shivered, remembering Mordecai's look when he had used that word.

The phone rang and I pulled my robe tighter as I went to the bedroom to answer it.

"Barb, I hope I'm not bothering you . . ."

Angel always called me Barb when she wanted something. With her ability to land on her feet, she had returned to her apartment after only one night at Mama and Daddy's. So I tried to imagine, as her voice flowed over the line, what she wanted.

"No problem, the kids are in bed. How are you?"

"Fine." Her voice was naturally rich and full, with a sensuous flow to it like honey. "Mama and Daddy, could you talk to them?"

"About?" At least I'd learned not to say yes right off.

"I'd like to bring a guest tomorrow night."

"Who?"

"I can't tell yet."

"Angel, if it is Madame Zsa Zsa, the answer is no."

"Oh, I hadn't even thought of her. Maybe she could come for dessert since she was so helpful to me in prison."

"Angel—"

"The guest is my fiancé, if you have to know, but I'm not telling you who. If you won't call them and ask, I'll do it myself."

She hung up the phone with the air of being put upon that only a youngest child can have. We, who had been at her beck and call in her youth, should be no different now. I went to the kitchen to find some Tylenol. I had a headache. It was there Edgar found me sitting, with my Diet Mountain Dew, when he got home.

The next morning the parade committee met at the Chamber of Commerce building. I arrived wearing my tree-ornament earrings, my mood lightened by the sunshine and soft breeze outside. All the parade details were checked and double-checked. To my relief, Bill Core was going to be Santa Claus this year. Philip Martin had pulled his back while rearranging the family room furniture, ending any thoughts of ho-ho-ho-ing for him. Viola sniffed at us as if we were at fault. We didn't tell him to put that Lazy Boy between the windows. My job was to make sure each float was in the correct place in line. For the *News Herald*, I was going to interview the Barefoot twins, Cora and Nora. They were Martinsboro's oldest citizens, ninety-eight years apiece, and were being honored as grand marshals of the parade.

After everyone left, I offered to walk Ladawn back down to the Victorian Room. It was time to live up to my promise to Bubba.

"Did Bubba mention our conversation to you?"

She teared up. "He told me everything. I cannot

believe he would do that to his own body. To put something like that in his system, to risk all there is, his health, his future."

"I know. I'm so sorry, but at least there is no permanent damage. The effects are reversible, especially no longer than he took the steroids. And he cooperated fully with J. C. and Agent Bailey, which should count for something."

She stopped and turned to me. "But he wasn't raised that way. He knows right from wrong. I did everything I could."

"Exactly, you did. He's an adult now. He has to make mistakes and learn from them."

"But when I think about poor little Martin—"

"Ladawn, he says he wasn't selling the stuff. I believe him. I think this whole thing will put him on the right track."

"I sure hope so. He really thinks you did a lot to keep him out of trouble. I can't tell you how much I appreciate it."

"I was at the right place at the right time to help him out. You'd do the same for one of mine."

She laughed. "Well, the good news is that since he is in the dog house, he can't do enough to help me out. Last night I came home and found the Christmas tree in the stand with the lights on it. He knows I hate to do that part. *And* he has volunteered to help with the Christmas parade."

"Gee, I wish he'd talk to my kids." Another possibility occurred to me. "Ladawn, do you think maybe he would be interested in going around and talking to high school kids? Dr. Patterson said that like one in fifteen high school guys uses steroids at some point."

"That's a great idea. When we get past the holidays we'll have to talk about it. Meanwhile, you are one of his favorite people in the whole world. He's sure you saved him from lifelong incarceration."

We parted ways and I went home to make a dozen recipes of two minute microwave fudge, as well as broccoli casserole and tarts. As I stirred powdered sugar and zapped butter, I worked on my questions for the next day's interview. Wiley and Manly kept coming to mind. Maybe I was wrong and the reverends wouldn't have had any reason to kill Wiley. Then again, he could have happened to be in the wrong place at the wrong time. Or maybe the reverends were lying about the drug operation. Maybe they were really a part of it. Both Mordecai and James had shown they wouldn't know the truth if it slapped them in the face. Three children aside, intuition only takes you so far when people can lie as easily as they can breathe.

And Bunny wasn't completely cleared in my mind. She's expecting. Manly's pushing her around. And she can't get a divorce before she starts showing; she'd lose everything like she lost her inheritance. That didn't explain what reason she would have for killing Wiley, but I still didn't know whose baby she was having. Maybe Wiley was the father and refused to marry her. *A little farfetched,* I thought to myself, *but it could have happened.* And the good madame. She had some sort of record. I knew that from J.C., but what kind? A petty thief does not a murderer make, necessarily. I came back to the reverends every time. Was it because they were the most likely candidates or because I thought they were scum of the earth?

When I got tired of chasing my tail on that issue, I tried to decide who Angel was marrying next. And where? And when? I'd liked it when she'd gone off with Larry to the Sugarland Wedding Chapel and got married. We had a reception for them when they got home. She always wanted the kids in the wedding, and those little dresses and suits could add up. I couldn't picture her marrying Buck, but stranger things had happened. If I hadn't been peeved at her for her call the night before I might have called and asked her a few more questions.

That evening, Edgar and I and the children managed with minimal screaming to arrive early at Mama and Daddy's. As usual, they had everything under control.

Vicki and Joe Dan arrived with Vicki all aflutter over the impending arrival of Dr. Merriwether. She was overdressed, and Joe Dan sulked, pulling at his necktie like it was a boa constrictor closing in on him. Vicki would have spent days preparing for this occasion; Mama set the same table for everyone. Any time guests were in for dinner was a notable occasion, and no one, by virtue of profession or anything else, received special treatment.

I rifled through a drawer, looking for a match for the candles. "Isn't Martin coming?"

Vicki adjusted the waistband of her pantyhose. "That Tiffany insisted on them going Christmas shopping tonight. I told her this was our family night, but Martin looked so pitiful. I told them not to worry about it, just to go on."

Misty Jane and Joshua Merriwether arrived next. Misty Jane seemed to float in; she was wearing a green velvet-and-taffeta dress. It had a sweetheart neckline, and the skirt stood out in a pouf all around her. I was reminded of dresses my Barbie Doll had worn. Misty Jane glowed. Joshua appeared to be reserving judgment on how he felt. He was dressed in a lavender button-down oxford shirt, no tie, and khaki Duck Head pants. We went through formal introductions even though everyone knew each other at least by sight. As we got to that awkward stage where everyone searches for something polite to say, Angel came in the door.

Angel is a theme dresser and she had chosen teal as her color. Her hair was french-braided with a teal ribbon winding through it. She had on a teal brushed-silk shirt, teal miniskirt, ribbed teal stockings, and teal cowboy boots. Behind her was Agent Bailey. For the life of me I couldn't figure why she'd invited him. He seemed his usual shifty self as she pulled him into the room.

"Everyone, I want you to meet my fiancé, Neal Bailey."

21

It was one of those moments when the silence seems to last for years. Twenty seconds stretched into twenty years. Mama reached the door and managed to hug both of them before the rest of us could even talk our feet into moving. Edgar shot me a look from the other side of the couch and I raised my eyebrows in return. I hugged Angel and offered her best wishes. I shook hands with Agent Bailey, Neal he was now, and offered him congratulations. I turned to go help Mama put the food out and realized Joshua Merriwether was standing beside Misty Jane giving Angel the once-over and not making much of an effort to disguise it. He realized I was watching him and looked away. Misty Jane was oblivious. Could Miss Hudson be right?

In short order steaming dishes and platters of chicken, turkey, and ham filled the table. In between were huge bowls of green beans, field peas, broccoli casserole, corn on the cob, and mashed potatoes. Edgar

called the children from the TV room and introduced
them to everyone, along with Daddy, who claimed a
first Nintendo victory over Jason.

We fell silent as Daddy asked for the Lord's blessings
on the food and the hands that prepared it. He said his
same blessing of the last thirty-five years, with a thank-
you added for Angel's release. Daddy's blessing, like
the doxology, made you feel connected to the ages.
Mama added hot biscuits to the table, and the clatter
of plates and utensils drowned out most of the conversation. Later, we adjourned to the living room, where
Mama's latest quilting project stretched across a
frame, her delicate stitches forming intricate patterns
on the fabric. The Upchurches, Alice and Reginald,
and Aunt Louise and Uncle Harvey were joining us for
dessert. I was closest to the door. There was a knock
and I jumped to open it, thinking they had arrived. In
front of me stood Madame Zsa Zsa. She was dressed in
her regulation caftan, looking much as I'd left her at
Manly's house. She must have come across a real deal
on caftans. This one was blue-green, giving an eerie
look to her eyes. She wore no coat and her caftan bil-
lowed out around her in the breeze, making me think
any minute the cat would come out from underneath
the edge of it into the house.

"Betsy, it is good to see you." She touched her cheek
to mine. Her skin felt oddly warm and leathery. A psychic with a bad memory.

"Barbara." I corrected her before Angel bounded
from the couch behind me.

"I'm so glad you came. I want you to meet Neal. It's
exactly like you predicted."

Aunt Louise and Uncle Harvey arrived a few minutes

later and knew my name. The Upchurches were on the porch before Aunt Louise and Uncle Harvey had their coats off, with Alice and Reginald bringing up the rear. Mrs. Upchurch brought her famous coconut creme pie. The other desserts were set out, looking like a smorgasbord of the "not allowed" foods on my last diet: pecan tarts, coconut cake, banana pudding, chocolate pecan pie, and Mississippi mud cake.

The children coming through to get dessert spotted Madame Zsa Zsa, and there was a great deal of peeking around doors and covert glances on walks back and forth between the kitchen and the TV room. This didn't bother Madame Zsa Zsa at all, and by the time she left she had given each of the girls a bracelet and Jason a polished stone she'd pulled from somewhere on her anatomy.

Neal Bailey took advantage of Angel's conversation with Madame Zsa Zsa to come over and stand beside me.

"J.C. tells me you think I'm a pretty sinister guy."

I felt my face coloring. "You certainly acted like one."

"I did and I apologize. You seemed to catch me every time I was down for a visit with Angel. First the night Wiley was hit and then when J.C. went back to search the Iron Body."

"It made me wonder. I figured you were a drug connection or something."

Now he seemed flushed. "I should have paid more attention to what was going on. I think we're developing some solid leads now. Your sister has a way of making me ignore my common sense."

"That's not all that unusual." He did seem happy

despite his initial reluctance to come into the house,
which I wrote off to nerves. He had been polite and
treated Angel, and indeed everyone, with a certain
respect, more than you could say for most of her
boyfriends, who assumed relatives were people you
went to see when you ran out of food and needed a
free meal.

Joshua Merriwether never looked Angel's way again
all night and went out of his way to be interested in
everyone. I soon decided I had read too much into the
look he'd given Angel earlier. He talked to Edgar and
me off and on all evening and was particularly interested in how things worked at the paper. He told us
what great children we had. I dismissed Miss Hudson's
comments as jealousy.

Joshua and Misty left early. Dating couples usually
like to have some time alone together, and the rest of
us left soon after, since most of us had some part to
play in the parade the next day.

As she was leaving, Madame Zsa Zsa took my hand to
say good-bye. I had decided live and let live. This was
not a night to hold grudges, but to celebrate. Madame
Zsa Zsa had announced shortly after discovering Neal
Bailey's line of work that Angel had free readings for
life. When Madame Z, as the kids had nicknamed her,
let go of my hand, her eyes rolled back and she
slumped to the floor, a sea of blue, green, and orange.
Only after much fanning and patting of washcloths did
the color in her face begin to return. Angel and Neal
insisted on driving her home before they took in a
movie, but as she left she came by, took my hand, and
whispered, "This only can I say: Do not go tomorrow."

Alice was standing beside me as Angel and Neal

helped Madame Z to the car. I offered her a refill on her coffee. "I told you she's something, didn't I? What could happen to me tomorrow? Nora Barefoot could hit me with her cane, I suppose."

Alice took my hand. "This only can I say: If you do not show up tomorrow, Ladawn and I will see to it that you have to watch CHOOSE GOD LTP Club reruns for a year."

My lip curled. "That's awful. Couldn't get much worse than that."

Understatement is a problem for me.

22

A *cold front moved* in overnight and we had to bundle up in the morning for the parade. It was only in the mid-forties, but there was a chilling wind, and our bodies had enjoyed sixty-degree temperatures only the day before; they were in rebellion. Edgar had agreed to get the children up and out, since I was going to have to leave the house at seven-thirty for my parade duties.

I suppose the cryptic little scene with Madame Zsa Zsa was rolling around in my subconscious somewhere, because I found myself pulling into the parking lot of the Iron Body at around seven-fifteen. I had no idea what I was looking for, but went around to the back by the exit everyone had used the night of the murder to get out of Manly's office. Nothing jumped out at me, nothing made me say aha, nor was I mystically drawn to the third Photinia bush to the right.

The coldness of the day made the landscape and the

building seem bleaker. I shouldn't even much care
who killed this man; if I was truthful with myself I
would say it didn't much matter, unless somehow I
could prove it was Mordecai and James and put them
away where they belonged.

I looked up and saw Mr. Otis McLamb coming
across the field. I had seen him too many times not to
stop and speak.

"Good morning. You're out mighty early."

He stuck his hands down in the pocket of his over-
alls. "I walk ever morning. I worked too many years to
be setting around waiting for Jesus to come. Takin it
easy, my boy says. Hogwash, I say. You're Charles and
Ruth Tew's girl aren't you?"

"Yes sir, I'm Barbara Gail."

His hand shook slightly as he held up three fingers.
"They had three girls, didn't they? I may be old, but
I'm not forgetful." He tapped his head. Without wait-
ing for me to answer, he went on. "Tell Charles and
Ruth I said hello."

"I'll do that. You tell Otis Jr. I said hello. I'm sure
the farm's a big job for him." I wasn't prepared for Mr.
McLamb's reaction.

"Ain't no such of a thing. I told him the other day.
Used to be farmers worked all the time. When we
wasn't planting and harvesting, there was trees to be
cutting and animals that needed lookin' after. Now-
adays, I told him, with all this fancy equipment he has,
he sits on his *A* double *S* from October to the next
spring."

"Is that right?" I was going to be late.

"Sure is, and I told him, furthermore, If you git sick,
don't go looking for none of your neighbors to come

about you at the hospital. Them days are gone.
Sometimes when I take my walk at night I look up at
the sky and wonder what the Lord must be thinking to
let the world git in such a mess as this."

"Mr. McLamb, do you walk every night?"

"Ever night unless it rains."

"Did you walk last Sunday night out this way?" I
pointed towards the Iron Body.

"Sure did."

"What time was it?"

"About nine-thirty. We'd had a bunch of company in
and they didn't leave till late, so I had to cut my walk
short to make it back for my favorite show, 'MacGyver.'
You ever watch 'MacGyver'? Course, it's reruns now."

"No, I can't say that I do. Were there any cars in the
parking lot then?" I was starting to sweat under all my
layers.

"There was two black ones. I remember cause one
was little and one was big and I thought they looked
like a mother and a baby."

"Do you remember what kind the big one was?"

"Not that I could swear to, one of those big fancy
new ones. It was polished up nice. I like it when people look after their automobiles. Shows character."

Wiley drove a little black car, the reverends drove a
big one.

"It's good to see you, Mr. McLamb. Tell everybody
hello and come see us." In Martinsboro, you told your
worst enemy and best friend, "Come see us."

I was ten minutes late, on Main Street, and had to
hustle to get the floats lined up. Ladawn had gotten red
visors for us all that said, PARADE STAFF, and I stuck mine
in my hair, oblivious to how it looked. I was walking on

air. At last, we had someone who could link Mordecai and James with Wiley and put them at the murder scene much earlier than they had said. I couldn't wait to get J. C. aside after the parade was over. I kept thinking that he would be around, but all the floats were in line and still there was no sign of him. I had to go interview Cora and Nora.

Cora and Nora were riding in a vintage Model-T. I decided five minutes into the interview that Nora was too mean to die and Cora wasn't going to do anything Nora didn't tell her to. When I asked what they attributed their longevity to Cora said, "I suppose God's so busy with more important things that he hasn't had time to bring us home yet." Nora let out a loud snort as comment.

I was turning to go when Ladawn came up carrying a cardboard box of Styrofoam coffee cups. Bubba was behind her, wearing a New Orleans Saints toboggan cap. "Glad to hear about your sister, Mrs. Upchurch." He pulled me to his shoulder in a sign of our new friendship.

I returned the hug. "Thanks. I'm relieved it's over." I was glad he hadn't seen his name on my list of suspects earlier.

Ladawn handed me a cup of coffee. "You want half-and-half?"

"No, thanks." I tucked my clipboard under my arm and cradled the cup in my gloved hands. "I may pour it on my toes."

"Be careful, it's steaming. Don't burn your tongue."

"Thanks for the warning." I opened the triangular plastic cutout in the lid, and steam rose off the top of the coffee and out into the air, leaving the smell behind as it evaporated. I turned to Ladawn. "Have you seen

J.C.? If he doesn't get here soon, he'll make everything late."

Custom was the chief's car came right before the grand marshall's, but it was nowhere to be seen.

She shook her head. "If you say anything to him, he growls."

"His bark's a lot worse than his bite."

Bubba pointed down the side street. "I'll go look for him this way."

"Thanks, Bubba, I'd really appreciate that." I walked up past the color guard hoping I'd spot Edgar and the kids as they came by. Alice, wearing a red visor, waved at me from her post by two troops of Brownies. She was responsible for merging the marching units in with the floats. I walked up to meet her.

"Well, girl, I'm sure glad to see you're not letting a little thing like a vision keep you at home."

"Day is not over yet, but I've got new information on the murder." I grinned at her. At that moment one of the tuba players down from us decided to test his horn. She shouted above the blast.

"I want to hear all as soon as this is over."

I nodded and went off towards the end of the street. I looked down into the parking lot of Martinsboro Savings and Loan. My heart felt like it rolled over. As alien looking as the first time I had seen it was the black BMW. It was parked off the entrance to White Street, which still contained a great deal of traffic, parents trying to park and walk their children over to the floats and marching units on the other street.

If the reverends had done Wiley in, maybe I could look at the bumper for damage. I looked around for a sign of Mordecai or James. Despite the latest round of negative press, the CHOOSE GOD organization had a massive float in the parade, complete with a live nativity scene. Mordecai and James were going to ride in two specially designed seats on the front, well away from the animals. Personally, I thought they would make a couple of great donkeys by the manger, but no one asked me. I looked at the car again. Pros and cons formed in my mind. The pros won. It couldn't hurt to walk over and take a peek. I looked up and down the street. No sign of the reverends.

The parking lot was empty except for an occasional family cutting across en route to the parade lineup. I went over and surveyed the front bumper head on. It looked like there might be a slight dent on the right-hand side. I assumed that was the side that hit Wiley. It was hard to tell. I moved closer. I bent farther down over the bumper; it was hard to bend over with all my layers on. I got down on one knee, carefully balancing my coffee so it wouldn't spill and burn my hand. A little more and I would be able to see the bottom.

Wiley had been killed wearing a fluorescent vest. I searched the bottom of the bumper. Was that a piece of fluorescent material stuck underneath? I reached my hand to try and grab it, thought better of it, and pulled my hand back. I moved slightly to the left to get a better view. If it was a piece of fluorescent cloth, J. C. would need to look at this anyway. I'd best let him pull it. I should tell him about it before the parade started. Two legs appeared in my vision, pieces of khaki cloth with loafer on the ends.

"Is there something I can help you with?"

That wasn't the voice of Mordecai or James. I realized I was holding my breath and let it out. Standing with care,

I looked into the smiling face of Joshua Merriwether. His smile made me pull my breath in again.

"Oh, no, I'm fine, really."

He said, "I've been afraid this was going to happen."

He didn't seem one bit afraid to me. "Is that right?" I was looking beyond him, off to the side, trying to spot Edgar or anyone I knew. Joshua's eyes made me nervous. I moved a step to the left. "Have you seen Edgar and the kids?"

He stepped right. "No, but I must tell you I have a gun in my pocket so, really, you'll need to be very careful what you do."

Fear froze the words in my mouth. I coughed, trying to unstick them. "It is a very dangerous thing to have a gun in a public place like this." I forced myself to breathe slowly like the Bradley method I'd used when I was having babies. *Try to sound calm and relaxed*, I thought.

He threw back his head and laughed. "Mrs. Upchurch, I'm well aware that you have finally put two and two together. One does not go around looking under the bumpers of people's automobiles for nothing."

I could feel my heart pounding erratically in my chest. The breathing was doing about as much good as it did when I'd had the children. "That's not true. I didn't even realize this was your car." I couldn't believe that I was going to die because I'd looked under the wrong car. It didn't matter to Joshua at this point that I had not a clue it was his BMW I was examining.

"By the way, there isn't anything underneath the bumper anyway. I cleaned it off."

Maybe I could play dumb. "Cleaned what off? And what's all this about a gun? For heaven's sake, my pen fell out of my hand and rolled under the car. I was trying to get it back. If you're this protective of a BMW, I'd hate to see you with a Rolls." I started to walk past him.

"Take another step, Mrs. Upchurch, and it may well be your last."

I stopped. Around the corner of the savings and loan, a child appeared. She was of grade school age, probably seven or eight, with long curly hair and hazel eyes that were more green than gray, as she approached. Details felt very big. I seemed to notice everything about her, as if she were the last child I would ever see. Her brown uniform hung from beneath her coat. One of the buttons on her blue coat was hanging by a thread.

"Can you tell me where I'm 'posed to be for the parade? It's time, and I'm going to miss it," she said.

Above her head, Joshua mouthed, "I'll kill her, too."

I didn't think he would risk a shot in this area unless he had to, but that offered me little consolation. There was no way I could take a chance that would cause this child to get hurt.

I pointed up the hill towards Alice. "That woman over there can help you. Would you please deliver a message for me?" Over her head I added, "She expects me to help her. Any minute she will send someone to get me. People could get hurt in the rush." Joshua nodded slightly at me. My hand was shaking. "Let me write it for you."

I cradled the clipboard in the crook of the arm that held my coffee. What could I write that would let Alice know I was in trouble? It had to be something

Joshua would not understand or he'd never let the little girl take it to her. I wrote:

> *Start without me. Make sure the band remem-*
> *bers to play "I've Got Confidence" for Cora and*
> *Nora.*
>
> *Barbara*

My signature was neat, very neat. Please let Alice
notice the signature that would have won me an *A* in
fourth-grade penmanship. The signature and the sig-
nificance of the song were all I had going for me. That
and Madame Zsa Zsa's warning. It was a stretch. At the
least, maybe she'd send somebody down to ask me
what was wrong.

Joshua read the note and nodded. I tore it from the
clipboard and gave it to the anxious child in front of
me. The child ran off in Alice's direction, smiling with
relief that she wouldn't miss the start of the parade.
The start of the parade that would be the end for me.
Once the parade started I couldn't count on anyone's
help. Underneath my clothes, sweat was trickling
down my sides and my back. My skin felt clammy.

I worked the top off my coffee cup, keeping my eyes
on Joshua's and away from my hands. I shifted, hoping
Joshua would shift so Alice wasn't in his line of vision,
and talked so he'd watch my mouth and not my hands.

"Ever treat anybody for ballistophobia?" He didn't
acknowledge my question, but looked past me toward
the parade. I didn't dare turn around to see if Alice
was reacting to my note. "That's the fear of bullets, you
know?" I laughed, shifting again as I did. What was
going on back there?

"One bullet could cure that."

"That's a case of the cure being worse than the disease, wouldn't you say?" I wanted to look behind me. Curiosity killed the cat. Curiosity killed the cat. I kept repeating that to myself.

Bubba Pittman came around the corner of the savings and loan.

"Mrs. Upchurch, I found Chief Spivey and he's moving his car into position. Parade should start right on time." He nodded at Joshua. "Hey Josh, how's it going man?"

Joshua licked his lip. "Great, you know, can't complain."

Water, water everywhere, and not a drop to drink. I kept trying to think of something I could do to draw Bubba's attention to the situation. It had to be subtle. If I did anything too overt, then Bubba would die, too.

Joshua was ahead of me. "I think someone just said your mother was looking for you."

Do something! Do something! the voice inside my head screamed to the rest of me. "Actually, I think she wanted you to help Alice out. She's needing extra hands with all those marchers." Joshua got behind Bubba. For a minute, I was afraid he wouldn't let him go. I willed Joshua to let him go.

"Right, there are a lot of little kids up there." He raised his hand to Joshua. "See ya, man. Take it easy." Bubba turned and started up the hill. Every step was good. It took him farther out of range.

Was Joshua crazy enough to shoot him? "Yeah, you too." Joshua turned back to me. My breath was coming in shallow spurts. Bubba moved out of range. *Breathe deep*, I told myself.

"Get in the car,. We're getting out of here." He pushed me towards the door.

I needed to stall. Could I faint? Would he shoot me if I did? If he shot me, what was going to happen to the kids? Edgar didn't even know everything they were going to get for Christmas. Was that why I'd been trying to get Edgar more involved? Did my subconscious know I was going to die? I wished it had shared that piece of information with the rest of me.

"Now." Joshua spat the word across the space between us.

In basketball, Dean Smith and the University of North Carolina made famous a stall called the Four Corners. You keep throwing the ball and moving so your opponents can't get it and score or foul you. They won a lot of games that way. I needed to think of a way to stall.

"Did you really kill them both?"

He laughed. "Of course I did. Manly and I had a good steroid operation going and he wanted to be piggish. People always want more. Everybody's greedy." No honor among thieves. "I'm not working in this hellhole the rest of my life to pay back a scholarship. So one quick knock on the head and it was over. I could find somebody else to peddle the stuff." His gesture was casual, like we were talking about Fuller Brush merchandise. "Once he was gone, Wiley started asking too many stupid questions. Then you scared him." This really seemed to annoy him. "You, as if you couldn't be taken care of. I told Manly we should have never cut Wiley in on it. Get in." He opened the door.

Another pass. Quick, he's coming for you. "I thought you only had to work three years to pay off your scholarship."

Again, that laugh that got tighter every time. "Sure, and while the rest of my classmates are setting up big-money practices in happening places, I'm going to lose three years of my life here. I spent the first twenty-five years with nothing and I promised myself I am never going to be that way again." I noticed that the number of people coming through the parking lot had slowed considerably. It was only the two of us.

He gestured with his pocketed hand towards the seat. "Quit dragging your feet."

The coffee lid was almost loose enough. Stall, throw the ball. Back at you. "Well, I have to know one more thing. What was your interest in poor Misty Jane?"

"God, what a zero that girl is. It killed me to have to be seen with her, but you're her aunt and I had to know what you knew. I listened to you talking to that Robocop your sister is going to marry last night and I knew I'd probably have to do this sooner or later."

He gestured impatiently towards the car's interior. "Get in now."

I touched the door. Even through my gloves, the handle felt cold and final. No more ways to stall. Nobody to throw the ball to.

"They are going to catch you. There is no way that you'll get away with all this."

"One thing's for sure, you won't be around to find out. Let's go."

"Hey girl, we're looking for you." Alice's voice came around the edge of the savings and loan. Joshua turned his head, realized he couldn't go both ways at once, and tried to lunge for me. His hand worked on getting the gun out of his pocket. Everything seemed magnified. I noticed in the moment that it took me to get the top off my coffee and sling it at his eyes that the gun must be tangled with the fabric of his pocket. I threw the clipboard after the coffee. His hands went to his eyes. I ran to the other side of the car. Someone was yelling, "Down! Down!" It sounded like J.C. I dived for the safety of shrubs, a high-pitched scream coming from my throat. I heard a warning yell and the sound of a shot and then profanity that gurgled in someone's throat. Shrub branches cut my face. Pain came from my leg. In my dive for the bushes, it had folded under me at an odd angle. I felt odd, like I was watching someone else burrowed there in the shrub. It was as if I was looking at someone else's leg.

Alice came around the corner of the car and had her arms around me. She was crying. I must have been crying, too, because my face was wet and tasted of salt.

Martinsboro News Herald
December 8, 1991

Martinsboro—The 12th annual Christmas parade was delayed this year due to a shooting that occurred shortly before the parade was to begin. Dr. Joshua Merriwether was treated and released into police custody for a gunshot wound to the arm. He was shot by Police Chief J.C. Spivey who had been alerted to a potential hostage situation by Alice Turner, a member of the *News Herald* staff. It has been confirmed that Dr. Merriwether will be charged in the murders of Manly Richards, a local businessman, and Wiley Bass, a member of the Martinsboro police force. (See related stories and pictures, page 2).

Epilogue

The related stories on page two were full of praise for Alice, Bubba, and J.C. Much as I like to think of myself as resourceful, my clever note alone would never have saved me. When Bubba went up the hill to tell Alice he was supposed to help her, she was still trying to figure out my note. He came up about the time that she'd decided to toss it. "Bubba, who is Barbara down there talking to anyway?" she had said to him.

"Dr. Merriwether."

"Well, he must be giving her some drugs then, cause this is the stupidest note I ever read."

That was the connection for Bubba. He finally realized who he'd seen Manly hanging out with, Joshua Merriwether. He'd come upon them one day in Raleigh eating lunch at the 42nd Street Oyster Bar. They had passed off their lunch together as happening to run into one another, which Bubba thought was a bit strange, but being Bubba he didn't give the subject much thought.

Alice sent Bubba after J. C. while she circled around to the other side of the savings and loan. Bubba used all those great running-back skills to get to J. C. right as he was getting his car into the parade lineup. They made it back to me just before Joshua Merriwether was going to sweep me off my feet. I have developed a whole new respect for jocks.

Tammy and Tina negotiated a settlement out of court for the damages incurred to their psyche. They can't tell what the six figures they each got are, but as my granddaddy used to say, "Everybody's business is nobody's damn business." To the twins' credit, they refused to settle unless Alice and I were left alone.

The criminal case against Mordecai and James was thrown out on a technicality. I wish I could say that people quit sending them and CHOOSE GOD money, but some people's need to belong is greater than their common sense.

Vicki is elated that Bubba has befriended Martin. The friendship helped get him through a tough time at school. Bubba's still working out, minus the steroids, hoping to walk on with the pros next spring.

Misty Jane was crushed about Joshua Merriwether's true intentions. She used her Christmas money this year to join a computer dating service in Raleigh. So far, according to Vicki, they have fixed her up with a dirt bike rider six years her junior and a car salesman who said he was a nonsmoker and then smoked all the way through dinner.

Angel and Neal Bailey are going strong, though she says they won't marry until at least the spring. Don't want to rush right into anything. Angel tells me she believes in short courtships and long engagements.

I've had time on my hands. My leg was broken in two places when I jumped into the bushes. The doctor tells me I'll take longer to heal considering my age and physical condition. For this I paid him money.

My leg breaking was not the only thing that happened in that moment when I was flying into the bushes. My thoughts were of lost chances, of Edgar and our children.

I realized, at the age of thirty-five, I had too much to do. You can't wait until tomorrow to live. Today may be it. I had physical therapy for my leg and spent the holidays on the couch or on crutches. Edgar pitched in and did all the holiday decorating, bought the majority of the Christmas gifts, made sure Melissa had the right color stockings to be an angel, that Jason didn't leave the house for the school program in last year's sneakers, and that Becky arrived in style for her first Christmas dance. When she left the house in her velvet and satin, I sat on the couch and cried.

Edgar did have some help, his mom and my mom. He insisted on doing the bulk of it himself, with the children assisting. I explained to him this still did not mean I wanted to occupy the same property as live chickens and pigs. I don't know how long the new Edgar will last, but it was nice to get a chance to know him.

From my vantage point on the couch, I could reach the phone. I investigated flying lessons, scuba instruction, and opening a bed-and-breakfast on the beach. My trip into the bushes taught me that you've got to stop and smell the roses, but it also taught me you've got to plant a few more varieties as well. I even called about that land Edgar wants. Becky will be driving in a few years anyway, so she could do some of the taxi service.

Christmas morning I unwrapped the biggest, gaudiest diamond anniversary ring I've ever seen. It was a band of diamonds, but it had one stone in the middle so big it didn't even look real. I was speechless. Edgar grinned at my surprise.

Then Martin arrived with Edgar's present from me, a puppy—redbone coonhound, of course. After the kids had gone off to their various pursuits, I hobbled, ring on my finger, over to sit next to Edgar. "Beautiful ring."

Over in the corner, Red, as he had been named, slept on a cedar-chip dog bed. He was worn out from three children's attention and in all the excitement had christened the family room rug in three spots.

"Great dog." Edgar kissed me, and I changed position to keep the pressure off my leg.

The question lay unspoken between us. I held up my hand catching the light with my ring. "I hate to sound unromantic, but how'd you pay for it?"

"I'll tell you tomorrow."

"No, better tell me today."

"Ninety days same as cash. I figured I'd cash in the CD we have at Martinsboro National."

I twirled it on my finger. "You mean the CD that I used as collateral for the loan I got at Martinsboro National to buy the dog? The loan I told them I'd pay off in ninety days so I could wait until after Christmas to get your signature without spoiling the surprise?"

Edgar's mouth hung open in a little *o*. "I suppose that would be the one."

I chuckled. "Oh, come on, you may as well laugh as

cry." Edgar started to laugh, and soon we were laughing so hard the movement was hurting my leg. Red opened one eye to make sure we weren't close enough to harm him.

"Would it bother you if I told you I think I'd rather have flying lessons than a ring?" I asked Edgar. "I imagine they are a lot cheaper."

"But you told me you wanted a ring. A token of my love for you that everyone could see."

I didn't want to tell him people on the West Coast could see this ring. What was a woman who drives a Taurus station wagon going to do with a ten-thousand-dollar ring?

"I changed my mind. What am I going to do with this ring? I know you love me. Maybe we could exchange it for a smaller one or wait until our twenty-fifth wedding anniversary and you can give me another one. For now I've got a lot more to do than flash a diamond band in front of every woman at the next mill social."

Edgar rolled his eyes. "That's what I'm afraid of."

After the Christmas parade caper, as Alice and I refer to it, she received a raise. I got a plaque. (That's what happens when you're part-time, no benefits.) It looks like Dr. Joshua Merriwether will be in prison a good while. The other day when Alice and I were eating danish and drinking coffee, she told me that she would have liked to have seen the look on Doris Hargrove's face when she realized that fish she thought she'd hooked for Marilyn was fried.

I laughed so hard I spilled coffee down the front of the white blouse the kids gave me for Christmas.

Glory in the Splendor of Summer with
101 Days of Romance

BUY 3 BOOKS —
GET 1 FREE!

Take a book to the beach, relax by the pool, or read in the most quiet and romantic spot in your home. You can live through love all summer long when you redeem this exciting offer from HarperMonogram.

Buy any three HarperMonogram romances in June, July, or August, and get a fourth book sent to you FREE!

Look for details of this exciting promotion in the back of each HarperMonogram published from June through August—and fall in love again and again this summer!

Evensong by Candace Camp

A tale of love and deception in medieval England from the incomparable Candace Camp. When Aline was offered a fortune to impersonate a noble lady, the beautiful dancing girl thought it worth the risk. Then, in the arms of the handsome knight she was to deceive, she realized she chanced not just her life, but her heart.

Once Upon a Pirate by Nancy Block

When Zoe Dunham inadvertently plunged into the past, landing on the deck of a pirate ship, she thought her ex-husband had finally gone insane and kidnapped her under the persona of his infamous pirate ancestor, to whom he bore a strong resemblance. But sexy Black Jack Alexander was all too real, and Zoe would have to come to terms with the heartbreak of her divorce *and* her curious romp through time.

Angel's Aura by Brenda Jernigan

In the sleepy town of Martinsboro, North Carolina, local health club hunk Manly Richards turns up dead, and all fingers point to Angel Larue, the married muscleman's latest love-on-the-side. Of course, housewife and part-time reporter Barbara Upchurch knows her sister is no killer, but she must convince the police of Angel's innocence while the real culprit is out there making sure Barbara's snooping days are numbered!

The Lost Goddess by Patricia Simpson

Cursed by an ancient Egyptian cult, Asheris was doomed to immortal torment until Karissa's fiery desire freed him. Now they must put their love to the ultimate test and challenge dark forces to save the life of their young daughter Julia. A spellbinding novel from "one of the premier writers of supernatural romance." —*Romantic Times*

Fire and Water by Mary Spencer

On the run in the Sierra Nevadas, Mariette Call tried to figure out why her murdered husband's journals were so important to a politician back East. Along the way she and dashing Federal Marshal Matthew Kagan, sent to protect her, managed to elude their pursuers and also discovered a deep passion for each other.

Hearts of the Storm by Pamela Willis

Josie Campbell could put a bullet through a man's hat at a hundred yards with as much skill as she could nurse a fugitive slave baby back to health. She vowed never to belong to any man—until magnetic Clint McCarter rode into town. But the black clouds of the Civil War were gathering, and there was little time for love unless Clint and Josie could find happiness at the heart of the storm.

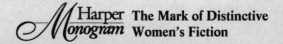

A little MURDER...

SUNRISE by Chassie West

Leigh Ann Warren returns to her hometown, Sunrise, North Carolina, to escape the harsh realities of being a big city cop. But the relaxation she seeks is soon marred by the discovery of a decades-old murder. Leigh Ann doesn't want to get involved, but the murderer strikes again, and this time it's too close to home to ignore.

TOO MANY COOKS by Joanne Pence

Mystery Scene calls this "a tasty little dish of suspense, romance and enough tart humor to please the most discriminating of tastes." Talk show host Angie Amalfi and her boyfriend, the gorgeous San Francisco homicide detective Paavo Smith, team up to investigate the suspicious death of a successful and much-envied restaurateur.

PEGGY SUE GOT MURDERED by Tess Gerritsen

M.J. Novak, a wisecracking, streetwise medical examiner, thinks she's seen it all until a red-haired woman named Peggy Sue mysteriously dies. Her suspicions lead her to Adam Quantrell, the sexy president of a pharmaceutical company. Together, they uncover corporate corruption, scandalous secrets, and sizzling romance.

NOTHING PERSONAL by Eileen Dreyer

From the award-winning, bestselling author of *If Looks Could Kill*. Burned-out critical care nurse Kate Manion wakes up from an accident in the worst possible place—the hospital where she works. Then her very own nurse, Attila the Buns, falls over dead, but it's no laughing matter. A serial killer is stalking the hospital staff, and one of Kate's friends may be the murderer.

 Available from HarperPaperbacks